THE PRODIGY

By the same author

Demian
Gertrude
The Journey to the East
Narcissus and Goldmund
Peter Camenzind
Siddartha

HERMANN HESSE
THE PRODIGY

Translated from the German by
W.J. Strachan

PETER OWEN
London and Chicago

PETER OWEN PUBLISHERS
81 Ridge Road, London N8 9NP

Peter Owen books are distributed in the USA and Canada by
Independent Publishers Group/Trafalgar Square
814 North Franklin Street, Chicago, IL 60610, USA

Translated from the German *Unterm Rad*

First British Commonwealth Edition 1961
This Peter Owen Modern Classic edition 2002
Reprinted 2014

© Hermann Hesse 1957

A catalogue record for this book is available from
the British Library.

ISBN 978-0-7206-1429-9

Printed and bound in Great Britain by
CPI Group (UK) Ltd, Croydon CR0 4YY

CHAPTER ONE

Herr Joseph Giebenrath, agent and dealer, had no special merits or peculiarities to distinguish him from his fellow citizens. He was possessed, like them, of a broad, healthy figure, tolerable business acumen, a sincere and undistinguished respect for money, a small private house with a garden, a family vault in the cemetery, a more or less unprejudiced, if threadbare attachment to the church, a proper respect for God and authority and a blind submissiveness before the inflexible decrees of middle-class respectability. He drank his share of beer but never got drunk. He embarked on more than one somewhat doubtful deal but never overstepped the bounds of strict legality. He referred deprecatingly to people poorer than himself as " starvelings " and the wealthier as " snobs." He was a member of the town council and took part in the skittle match in the " Eagle " every Friday and also sampled the hors-d'oeuvre and sausage soup when " Baking Day " came round. In the office he smoked cheap cigars, reserving a superior brand for after dinner and Sundays.

His inner life was in every respect that of a philistine. The more sensitive side of his character had long been overlaid with the dust of neglect and now consisted of little more than the traditional rough and ready acknowledgement of the family, pride in his son and an occasional generous impulse towards the poor. His intellectual prowess did not extend beyond his innate but narrowly circumscribed cunning and a certain dexterity with figures. His reading was confined to the Newspaper and for amusements the annual performance by the town club amateur theatricals and a visit to the circus in between times made up all he demanded from the world of entertainment.

He could have exchanged his name and dwelling with any one of his friends without its making the slightest difference. He even shared his inmost soul, his watchful distrust of every superior power and personality, and his jealous hostility towards anything unusual, less hidebound, anything that was intellectual with every other paterfamilias in the town.

Enough of him. It would require a profound satirist to deal with his humdrum existence and its unconscious tragedy. But this man had a son and of him there is more to say.

Hans Giebenrath was certainly a gifted child; you could see at a glance how distinguished and different he was as he moved about among the other boys. This small place in the Black Forest had not produced anybody like him before; so far no man had ever gone forth from there into the world whose horizon or activity had transcended the most ordinary limits. It was impossible to say where the boy had got his serious eyes, intelligent brow and superior gait. From his mother perhaps. She had been dead some years and no one had noticed anything special about her during her lifetime beyond the fact that she had been perpetually ailing and worried. The father did not come into it. The mysterious spark from above had then for once descended into this out of the way place which in the eight or nine centuries of its existence had brought forth so many worthy citizens but never anything exceptional by way of talent or genius.

An intelligent modern observer, remembering the

weakly mother and taking into account the considerable age of the family, might have had something to say about the hypertrophy of the intellect as a symptom of incipient degeneration. But the town was fortunate enough not to harbour any people of that kind, and only the younger and shrewder among the civil servants and schoolmasters had acquired even a sketchy knowledge of "modern man" from newspaper articles. It was possible to live and be brought up there without any familiarity with the discourses of Zarathustra; marriages were respectable and frequently happy and the whole of life followed an incorrigibly old-fashioned pattern. The prosperous, comfortably established citizens, many of whom had graduated from the artisan to the manufacturing class during the last twenty years, certainly doffed their hats to officials and sought their company but among themselves referred to them as starvelings and pen-pushers. Oddly enough, however, they recognized no greater honour than that of allowing their own sons to study and become officials should the opportunity offer. Unfortunately this remained virtually a blissful but empty dream for new blood found its way there chiefly through the schools with a classical bias and even then only after much sweat and repetition of work.

There was no doubt about Hans Giebenrath's talents. The masters, headmaster, neighbours, the local vicar, his fellow-pupils, everybody in fact agreed that the boy had a fine and quite exceptional intellect. His future course was therefore already fixed and mapped out. For in Swabia talented boys—provided their parents could afford it— there was but one narrow path and it was to the Seminary by way of the *Landexamen* and thence to the Protestant Theological College at Tübingen and from there either to

7

the pulpit or the lecturing desk. Three or four dozen boys from the province of Wurtemberg tread this quiet, untroubled path every year; thin, newly-confirmed, overworked they cover the various territories of humanistic knowledge at the State's expense and eight or nine years later embark on the second, in most cases longer part of their lives during which they are expected to repay the State for the benefits received.

Once again the *Landexamen* was due to take place in a few week's time. It was the name chosen to designate the annual hecatomb when the State selected the finest intellectual flower of the Province and during which time prayers and wishes of innumerable families were directed from the townships and villages towards the county town where the examination was held.

Hans Giebenrath was the sole candidate whom the little town considered worth sending up for the painful ordeal of this competitive examination. It was a great but by no means undeserved honour. An extra Greek lesson with the Headmaster was added to his ordinary class work which lasted up to four o'clock in the afternoon; at six, the vicar was good enough to give him a revision period in Latin and divinity and twice a week he had an hour's coaching from the mathematics master after supper. In Greek, next to the irregular verbs, the main emphasis was laid on variety of sentence structure expressed through the use of particles, in Latin they were expected to concentrate on clear and precise statements, and become familiar with countless refinements of prosody, in mathematics pride of place was given to complicated problems in arithmetic. None of these things, as his teacher was never tired of repeating, had any apparent value for his later studies, but it was only " apparently," for in point of fact, they were very important indeed, more important than many main subjects because they developed the logical faculties and formed a basis for all clear, sober and cogent reasoning.

In order to safeguard Hans against excessive mental fatigue and prevent the spiritual side of his character from languishing through neglect, he was allowed to attend confirmation classes every morning, one hour before school, when a refreshing breath of religious life from the Brenze catechism and the stimulating learning by heart of questions and responses might pervade his and other youthful souls present. But, alas, he ruined these hours of spiritual refreshment for himself and deprived himself of any blessing he might gain, for he surreptitiously hid sheets of paper in his catechism together with Greek and Latin word-lists or exercises and busied himself with this worldly knowledge practically the whole hour. Yet his conscience was never blunted enough to prevent his continually feeling a guilty uneasiness and slight anxiety. If the chaplain approached him or called out his name, he would start nervously, and when he had to give an answer his brow was covered with sweat and his heart beat fast. But his replies were invariably correct and faultlessly expressed and his teacher was highly gratified.

His written or learning work which accumulated daily from one lesson to the next could then be done late into the evening at home by cosy lamplight. This quiet work in an atmosphere of domestic peace to which his form-master ascribed a particularly profound and stimulating effect did not normally extend beyond 10 p.m. on Tuesday and Saturday but on the other evenings he was up until 11.0, midnight and sometimes even later. Although his father grumbled a little about the extra consumption of oil, he regarded this studying with pleasurable pride. For the few leisure hours and Sundays—which, after all, make up a seventh part of our lives—he was strongly urged to read authors not studied in school hours and revise the grammar rules. " In moderation, of course ! A walk once or twice a week is necessary for health and will do you a power of good. When the weather permits you can take a book out into the fresh air with you—you will find how easy and pleasant it is to learn things in the open air. Above all, keep your chin up ! "

So Hans kept his chin up to the best of his ability and from this time on he used his walks for purposes of study and went about shy and reserved, his face drawn from his late nights and dark rings under his tired eyes.

" What do you think of Giebenrath; will he pull it off ? " said his form-master one day to the Headmaster.

" Certainly he will," replied the latter cheerfully. " He's exceptionally talented; you have only got to see him. He has an ethereal look about him."

The degree of etherealization had become startling during the previous week. Restless eyes with a melancholy light burned in his handsome boyish face, his noble brow was furrowed with fine wrinkles that spoke of much thought, and his slender delicate arms and hands hung down by his sides with the tired gracefulness of a Botticelli figure.

It had come to the stage when Hans was to set off next day for Stuttgart with his father and prove in the *Land-examen* whether or not he was worthy to enter the narrow gates of the Theological College. He had just had a parting interview with his headmaster.

" You are not to do any more work to-night," said that awe-inspiring gentleman with unwonted mildness. " Promise. You must arrive absolutely fresh in Stuttgart to-morrow morning. Go for an hour's stroll and then get to bed in good time. Young people must have a good night's rest."

Hans was astonished at all this solicitude on his behalf instead of the dreaded outpouring of good advice, and he gave a sigh of relief as he left the school building. The tall Kirchber lime trees glowed softly in the warm late afternoon sunshine and the water in the two large fountains in the market place splashed and glistened; the deep blue of the nearby pine forest showed above the irregular line of the receding roofs. Hans felt as if an age had gone by since he had last set eyes on this sight and its attraction and beauty struck him with unaccustomed force. It was true that he had a headache, but at least he had not to learn any more that day.

He slowly made his way across the market place, past the old town hall, through the Marktgasse and along by the cutler's to the old bridge. There he strolled up and down for a time and finally sat down on the broad parapet. Four times a day for weeks and months he had walked past this spot and had had no eyes for the small gothic chapel on the bridge nor for the river nor the sluice, the weir and the mill—not even for the bathing meadow and the willow-grown bank along which was a whole succession of tanneries where the river stood deep and green and as tranquil as a lake and where the arching willow branches hung down into the water.

He now realized how many half and whole holidays he had spent here, how often he had swum, dived, rowed and fished at this place. Oh, the fishing! He had almost forgotten everything he knew of that sport and during the past year he had wept bitterly when it had been forbidden on account of his examination. Fishing had been the best

11

thing in the whole long school year. Standing there in the light shadow of the willows, with the murmur from the nearby mill weir, the deep quiet water ! And the play of light on the river, the gentle bending of the long fishing rod, the excitement at the bite and the winding-in and the special thrill when you held a cool, fat wriggling fish in your hand !

He had pulled out many a tender carp, dace and barbel; delicate tench, too, and tiny, prettily-coloured minnows. He gazed over the water for some time, and at the sight of this whole stretch of green river he became thoughtful and sad, conscious that the lovely, free, irresponsible pleasures of boyhood lay far behind him. He pulled a lump of bread mechanically out of his pocket, rolled large and small pellets which he threw into the water and watched them sink and get snapped up by the fish. First the tiny minnows and carp came up and greedily consumed the smaller pieces, pushing the larger pieces before them in zigzag fashion. Then a larger dace swam up slowly and cautiously, its broad dark back rose feebly from the bottom, circled thoughtfully round the pellets which were suddenly engulfed in its round gaping mouth. A warm, damp smell rose from the lazily flowing river; a few bright clouds were vaguely reflected in the green surface; the circular-saw whined in the mill and from both weirs came the low chuckle of cool, rushing water. Hans' thoughts went back to the Sunday of his recent confirmation during which, right in the middle of all the excitement and solemnity he had caught himself out memorizing a Greek verb. It had often happened like that latterly; his mind would go off on to something else, and even in class he was always thinking about a former or future piece of work instead of the matter in hand. It would be wonderful in the exam !

Distracted, he stood up, undecided where to go next. It gave him quite a start when a powerful hand fell on his shoulder and a friendiy voice said, " Good day, Hans, coming along a short way with me ? "

It was the shoemaker, Flaig, at whose house—though not for some time now—he had spent the occasional odd hour in the evening in the old days. Hans walked along with him but had only half an ear for what the pious lay preacher had to say. Flaig was discussing the examination; he wished Hans luck and spoke words of encouragement. But the main drift was that examinations of this sort were outside the normal routine and that failure in them was no disgrace; it might happen to the best, and if he should be unlucky, he was to remember that God had special plans and a path marked out for each soul.

Hans' conscience was not altogether clear concerning Flaig. He had a great respect for his sound and impressive character, but he had heard so many jokes—in which he had joined, often against his better judgment—about lay-preachers; furthermore he felt ashamed of his cowardice because, for a considerable while now, he had been avoiding the shoemaker, frightened of his shrewd questions. Since the time when Hans had begun to be the pride of his teachers and a little priggish perhaps, Flaig had given him such a curious look. The boy had gradually escaped the hold of his well-meaning mentor, for Hans was in the stage of adolescent defiance and his antennae were sensitive to any interference with his personality. He was now striding along by his side, oblivious of the anxious and kindly looks Flaig was bestowing on him.

In the Krongasse they met the vicar. The shoemaker

gave him a cool, formal greeting and suddenly put on a spurt, for the vicar—according to rumour—was one of the new school of thought and reputed not to believe even in the Resurrection. But he took the boy along with him.

" How are you doing ? " he asked. " You will be feeling relieved to have got to the present stage."

" Yes; very glad."

" Well, don't worry. You know we have high hopes of you. I am expecting a particularly good performance from you in Latin."

" But supposing I fail," said Hans timidly.

" Fail ? " The vicar stood there, completely taken aback. " Failure is simply impossible. Quite impossible. What an idea ! "

" I only mean that it might happen . . ."

" It can't, Hans, it can't; don't worry about that. And now give your father my best wishes and cheer up."

Hans followed him with his eyes; then he looked round for the shoemaker. What had *he* said ? It did not matter as much as all that about Latin, provided you had your heart in the right place and feared God. It was easy for him to talk. And now the vicar. He could never face him if he failed.

Depressed, he crept home and into the steep little garden. A tumbledown summerhouse stood there which had long been out of use; he had knocked up a wooden hutch in it in the old days and had kept rabbits for three years. They had been taken away from him the previous autumn because of the examination. He had no longer any time for such distractions.

He had not even been in the garden for a long time now. The empty grotto looked dilapidated; the cluster of stalactites in the corner had collapsed, the little wooden water wheel lay warped and broken beside the conduit. He thought back to the time when he had sawn it all out and built it up and the fun he had derived from it. It was two years ago—an eternity. He picked up the wheel, bent it back, broke it in two and threw it over the fence. Away with the toy, it was all finished with long ago. At that point he remembered his school friend August. It was he who had helped him build the water-wheel and patch up the rabbit hutch. Whole afternoons they had played here; shot with a catapult, ambushed cats, erected tents and eaten raw carrots for supper. Then the days of serious work had begun and August had left school, a year ago now, and become an apprentice mechanic. He had only shown up on two occasions. He too had no more time, now.

Cloud shadows raced over the valley; the sun was already sinking towards the mountain ridge. For a moment Hans felt he must throw himself down and weep aloud. But instead he fetched the axe from the shed and swung it through the air with his thin arms and smashed the rabbit hutch to pieces. The splinters flew, the nails bent with a squeak, a small quantity of rotted rabbit food, left over from the previous summer came to light. He threw everything away as if by so doing he hoped to kill the longing he still felt for the rabbits and August and all the old childish games.

" Now, now, what's going on there ? " his father called out from the window. " What are you up to ? "

" Chopping firewood."

He made no further reply but threw down the axe and ran through the yard, up the lane and followed the bank upstream. Outside, close to the brewery were two moored rafts. In the old days he had often floated downstream for hours on warm afternoons, lulled and excited at the same time by the journey over the water that lapped against the tree-trunks. He jumped across on the loose floating logs, lay down on a clump of osiers and tried to imagine that the raft was floating now quickly, now slowly past meads and fields, villages and cool forest fringes, under bridges, through open locks and that he was lying on it and everything was as it used to be when he collected rabbit food in the Kapfberg, fished by the river bank in the tanner's garden and had no headaches or worries to put up with.

Tired and listless he made his way homeward for supper. His father was enormously excited about the journey to Stuttgart for the examination and asked over and over again whether the books were packed, whether he had put out his black suit, whether he wanted to study his grammar en route, whether he felt in good form. Hans gave short, laconic replies, ate very little and soon said goodnight.

" Goodnight, Hans. Mind you sleep well ! I'll wake you at six then. You haven't forgotten your dictionary, have you ? "

" No, I have not forgotten the *lexicon*. Goodnight ! "

He lay awake for long enough without a light in his little room. It was the only blessing this examination business had brought him so far — his own small room in which he could be undisturbed and was answerable to no one. Here he had brooded long evening hours—obstinate, defiant and ambitious—battling with weariness, sleep and headache over Caesar, Xenophon, grammars, dictionaries and mathematical problems, often on the point of despair. Here he had also passed the few hours which were worth more than all the vanished pleasures of boyhood, those few, magically rare hours, full of pride and excitement and triumph when he dreamed and wished himself far away from school, examinations and all the rest, and transported to a circle of higher beings. Then he was seized by the bold, blissful consciousness that he was truly of different stuff—better than his fat-cheeked, good-natured companions and perhaps one day he would look down on them from a superior height. Even at the present time he took a deep breath as if a freer, cooler air circulated in this room than elsewhere, sat down on the bed and passed a few twilight hours in dreams, hopes and longings. Slowly his delicate eyelids drooped over his large, overtired eyes, opened again, blinked and then fell; his pale, boyish head sank on to his lean shoulders, his slender arms stretched out wearily. He had fallen asleep while still fully dressed, and the tender, maternal hand of sleep soothed the surging waves in his restless boyish breast and erased the tiny wrinkles from his handsome forehead.

It was amazing. The vicar had taken the trouble to go along to the station despite the very early hour. Herr Giebenrath stood stiffly in his black frockcoat, unable to keep still for excitement, pleasure and pride; he trotted nervously round the headmaster and Hans, acknowledged all the messages wishing them "a good journey" and "the best of luck" to his son in the examination on the part of the station officials, and he gripped his small suitcase, first in his left, then his right hand. One moment he held his umbrella under his arm, the next, wedged it between his knees, dropped it several times and then deposited it on the ground only to pick it up again. You would have thought that he was undertaking a journey to America and not merely to Stuttgart and back. His son appeared outwardly quite calm though he felt choked by a secret apprehension.

The train arrived and stopped; the passengers mounted; the Headmaster waved his hand, his father lit a cigar and the town and river disappeared from view in the valley below. The journey was a torment for both of them.

His father suddenly perked up when they got to Stuttgart and began to become cheerful and affable again; he showed all the excitement of the small townsman who has come up to the county town for a few days. Hans became more anxious and quiet; he felt a deep constriction inside him as he got his first view of the town; the strange faces, the vulgar, over-ornate houses, the long, tiring streets, the horse-trams and the noise of the traffic intimidated and distressed him. He was put up at an aunt's where the strange rooms, his aunt's cheerful loquacity, the long, aimless sitting around and never-ending remarks of encouragement from his father utterly depressed him. Feeling odd and out of place, he sat down in the room, and when he looked at the unaccustomed surroundings, his aunt and her townish clothes, the carpet with its large pattern, the mantelpiece clock, the pictures on the wall or—through the window—the noisy streets, he felt somehow betrayed and had the impression of having been away from home for an eternity and having entirely forgotten all the knowledge which he had so painfully acquired.

He had intended to run through his Greek particles in the afternoon, but his aunt suggested going for a walk. A prospect of green meadows and the murmur of trees rose momentarily before Hans' inner eye and he cheerfully consented. Soon, however, he realised that even a walk was a different sort of pleasure here in the great city from what it was at home.

He went alone with his aunt since his father was paying visits in the town. His trials began as soon as he put his foot on the stairs. They encountered a fat, pompous-looking lady to whom his aunt curtsied and began to chatter with great volubility. They were held up for more than a quarter of an hour. Meantime Hans leant against the bannisters, was sniffed and growled at by the lady's dog and became vaguely aware that they were talking about him, for the fat stranger looked him up and down repeatedly through her pince-nez. Hardly had they got into the street when his aunt entered a shop and it was some time before she returned. Meantime Hans stood shyly in the street, jostled by passers-by and jeered at by street boys. When his aunt emerged, she handed him a bar of chocolate and he thanked her politely although he did not like chocolate. They got into a horse-tram at the next street-corner and now they rattled down the never-ending streets in this overcrowded vehicle to the accompaniment of a continuous bell-ringing until they finally reached a broad avenue and ornamental park. Through it ran a stream, fenced-in flower beds were in full bloom and goldfish swam in a small artificial pond. They wandered up and down, to and fro and round and round among a host of pedestrians like themselves and saw a crowd of different faces, and smart clothes, bicycles, invalid-chairs, perambulators, heard a babel of voices and inhaled a warm, dusty air. At length they sat down on a bench next to some other people. His aunt never stopped talking. Now she sighed, smiled amiably at her nephew and invited him to eat his chocolate. He had no desire to. " For heaven's sake ! You're not going to be awkward, are you ? Just eat it up."

Then he extracted the tablet from his pocket, removed

a corner of silver paper and finally bit off a very modest piece. He hated chocolate although he did not dare confess as much to his aunt. While he sucked the small piece and was trying to swallow it down, his aunt had discovered an acquaintance in the crowd and was rushing off.

" Sit here. I'll be back in a moment."

Hans took his opportunity and flung his bar of chocolate as far as he could on to the lawn. Then he swung his legs to and fro, staring at all the people and felt miserable. In the end he began to go over his irregular verbs but was horrified to discover that they had practically gone out of his head. He had clean forgotten them. And tomorrow it was the *Landexamen*.

His aunt returned, having meantime collected the information that this year there were one hundred and eighteen candidates. The boy's heart sank into his boots and he did not say another word all the way back. His headache returned once he was in the house and he had no appetite for any food; he went about so depressed that his father spoke to him severely and even his aunt thought he was behaving in an insufferable manner. He fell into a deep but restless sleep, haunted by nightmarish scenes. He saw himself sitting in the examination hall with the one hundred and seventeen other candidates; the examiner who at first resembled the vicar at home and then his aunt, piled up mountains of chocolate before him which he was expected to eat. And as he ate, with eyes full of tears, he saw the others stand up one after the other and vanish through a little door. They had all consumed their mounds of chocolate but his own grew higher and higher as he watched, flowed over table and desk as if it would suffocate him.

Next day as Hans was drinking his coffee without daring

to take his eyes off his watch for fear he should be late for his exam, he was in many people's thoughts in his home town. Especially shoemaker Flaig's. The latter was saying prayers before breakfast with the members of his family and his assistants and both apprentices standing in a circle round the table and to his usual morning prayer the shoemaker added the words: " O Lord, watch over the schoolboy Hans Giebenrath also who is sitting for an examination to-day; bless and fortify him so that he may one day become a strong and fearless proclaimer of Thy Holy Name ! "

The vicar if he did not actually pray for him, remarked to his wife at breakfast: " Giebenrath will be just entering the examination hall. He'll do something remarkable; they are bound to notice him and then it won't do me any harm that I helped him with his Latin."

Before the lesson, his form-master said to his pupils: " Well, the *Landexamen* will be on the point of starting in Stuttgart and we must wish Giebenrath the best of luck. Not that he needs it — he's worth ten lazybones like you put together ! " And even most of the boys were now thinking of the absent pupil or, at any rate, a considerable number of them had laid bets with each other on his success or failure.

And as sincere intercession and inner sympathy can effectively bridge great distances, Hans, too, was aware that they were thinking about him at home. Indeed, he entered the examination hall, accompanied by his father, with wildly beating heart and nervous and frightened followed the invigilator's instructions and gazed round the large room filled with pallid boys as if he was a criminal in the torture-chamber. But when the professor arrived and ordered silence and dictated the text for the Latin stylistic paper, Hans, who was breathing hard, found it child's play. Quickly, almost joyfully, he made his rough copy, transcribed it neatly and carefully and was one of the first to hand in his version. It is true that he lost his way home to his aunt's and wandered round the sweltering streets for two hours but even that did not unduly upset his newly-regained composure; he was only too glad to escape from his aunt and his father for a while and stroll through the noisy residential quarter like a bold explorer. When by dint of much inquiry he had found his way back, he was bombarded with questions.

"How did it go? What was it like? Did you know your stuff?"

"It was easy," he said proudly, "I could have translated it when I was in the third form."

And he ate with a hearty appetite.

He had no examination in the afternoon. His father dragged him round to some friends and relations. At one of their houses, they met a timid boy in a black suit who likewise had come for the *Landexamen*—in his case, from Göppingen. The grown-ups left the boys to themselves and they looked at each other with shy curiosity.

"How did you get on with the Latin? Easy, wasn't it?" asked Hans.

"Terribly easy. But it's always like that; you always make the most slips in the easiest papers. You get careless. There were sure to have been some hidden snags."

"Do you think so?"

"Of course. The examiners aren't fools."

Hans was rather frightened and grew pensive. Then somewhat faint-heartedly he asked, "Have you got the paper there?"

The boy produced his exercise-book and they both

worked through the whole piece word by word. The Göppingen candidate seemed to be an expert latinist—at least he trotted out twice grammatical designations Hans had never heard of.

" And what's on to-morrow ? "

" Greek and essay."

Then the Göppingen boy inquired how many candidates Hans' school had put in.

" Just me," said Hans, " no one else."

" Oh, there are twelve of us from Göppingen ! Including three brilliant candidates who are expected to win the first places. Last year the first was one of us, too. Are you going to a Grammar School if you fail ? "

The point had never been discussed.

" I don't know . . . No, I should doubt it."

" Really ? I am going on with my studies in any case, even if I fail now. My mother will send me to Ulm."

This impressed Hans very much. He also felt very nervous about the dozen candidates from Göppingen with their three particularly brilliant boys. He could not bear to show himself any more.

He sat down when he got home and revised the Greek verbs in " mi." He had no fears about the Latin; he felt on safer ground in that subject. But he had a special feeling about Greek. He liked Greek; it was almost a passion of his but only as far as reading was concerned. Xenophon for example was so finely, so movingly written, so fresh; it sounded gay, attractive and powerful; it had a light-hearted spirit about it and was easy to follow. But once grammar came into it or he had to translate from German into Greek he was lost in a maze of conflicting rules and usages and he felt almost the same anxious timidity before this foreign language as he had felt during

23

the very first lesson when he could not even read the Greek alphabet.

Next day was Greek, followed by German essay. The Greek was fairly long and by no means easy; the essay subject difficult and somewhat ambiguously couched. From 10 o'clock on it became hot and stuffy in the hall. Hans had a faulty pen-nib and ruined two sheets of paper before completing the fair copy of his Greek. While doing the essay he was driven nearly frantic by an importunate neighbour who thrust a piece of paper at him containing a question and nudged him to try and force him to answer. Communication with neighbours was strictly forbidden and, if discovered resulted in disqualifying the candidates involved without any right of appeal. Trembling with fright, Hans wrote "Leave me alone" on the paper and turned his back on the questioner. And it was so hot. Even the supervisor who walked up and down the hall with measured tread, never pausing, passed his handkerchief several times over his face. Hans sweated in his thick "confirmation" suit, contracted a headache and finally handed in his papers, feeling far from happy and convinced that they were full of mistakes and that he had now completely spoilt his chances as far as the examination was concerned. He did not speak at table, content to shrug his shoulders when they questioned him; he might have almost committed some crime to judge by the expression on his face. His aunt said some words of comfort but his father got up, thoroughly annoyed with him. After supper he took the boy into the next room and tried to wring replies out of him.

"It was awful," said Hans.

"Why didn't you take the proper trouble? Surely you can take a grip of yourself. Damn it all!"

Hans fell silent and when his father began to curse, he blushed and said. " You don't know anything about Greek ! "

The worst of it was that he had a " viva " coming on at 2.0 p.m. It was this part of the exam that terrified him most. He felt utterly miserable on his way there through the hot streets, and he could hardly see out of his eyes for fear and giddiness. A full ten minutes he sat at a long green-covered table in front of three men, translated a few Latin sentences and answered the questions put to him. For a further ten minutes he sat before three different men, translated a Greek passage and was again questioned. Finally they wanted to know an irregular aorist but he could not answer.

" You can go now—that way, the door on the right."

He went but just as he reached the door, the aorist came back to him. He stood still.

" Go along," they called out, " go along ! Or are you feeling unwell ? "

" No, but the Aorist had suddenly come back to me."

He shouted it into the room, saw one of the men laugh and then he darted off, his head on fire. Then he tried to think of the questions and his answers, but everything seemed in a whirl. The large green table surface, the three serious old men in their frock coats swam before his eyes, the open book and his own trembling hand laid on it. Heavens above, what sort of replies must he have given !

As he strode through the streets, he felt as if he had been there for weeks and would never be able to get away again. The image of his father's garden, the hills blue with pine-trees, the fishing spot by the river all seemed remote, like something seen long ago. If he could only go home to-day! It wasn't any use staying any longer; in any case he had ploughed his exam.

He bought himself a milk roll and wandered round the streets the whole afternoon in order not to have to put up with his father's questions. When he finally arrived home, they had been getting worried about him, and as he looked depressed and exhausted, they gave him broth with an egg in it and packed him off to bed. Next day it was mathematics and divinity, then he could return home. The following afternoon things went smoothly enough. It was bitterly ironical to Hans that everything should go well that day after his confounded bad luck in the main subjects. The chief point now was to get away, to get home!

"The exam is over; we can go home now," he announced to his aunt.

His father wanted to go to Cannstatt and drink coffee in the Kurgarten. However, Hans pleaded so urgently that his father allowed him to travel back alone, escorting him to the train. Hans was kissed by his aunt, was given his ticket and something to eat and feeling exhausted, his mind a blank, he travelled homeward over the green, mountainous land. Only when the blue-black Tannenberge rose up before him did a feeling of joy and relief come over him. He thought with pleasure of their old housemaid, his little room, the Headmaster, and the familiar, low schoolroom and all the other things.

Luckily there were no inquisitive acquaintances at the station and he was able to hurry home unnoticed with his small bundle.

"Was it nice in Stuttgart?" asked old Anna.

"Nice? Do you think an exam can be nice? I'm just glad to be back here again. Father isn't coming until to-morrow."

26

He drank a bowl of fresh milk, collected his bathing trunks which were hanging in front of the window and ran off, but not to the meadow where all the others went to bathe. He went a long way out of the town to the *Waage* where the river flowed deep and slowly between tall-growing scrub. There he undressed, tested the cool water first with his hand, then his foot, shivered a little and then made a sudden plunge into the water. He felt the sweat and anxiety of the last few days slip off him as he breasted the weak current. The river took his slender body in its cool embrace and he was conscious of a fresh affection for his beautiful native town. He swam more quickly now, rested, swam again and revelled in the exquisite coolness and fatigue that took possession of him. Turning on to his back, he let himself float downstream again, listened to the high-pitched whine of the midges swarming in golden circles, and looked up at the late-evening sky which was continually intersected by darting swallows and rose-tinted by a sun that had already disappeared behind the mountains. When he was dressed again and strolling home dreamily, the valley was already full of shadows.

He walked past the garden of Sackmann the shopkeeper which he had once robbed of some unripe plums with a gang of other small boys, and into the Kirchner timber-yard where the white pine planks lay around under which he had always found his worms for bait in the old days. He went on past Inspector Gessler's cottage; it was his daughter Emma whom he would so willingly have made the object of his attention two years before on the ice. She had been the daintiest and best-dressed schoolgirl in the town and his own age; at that time there had been nothing in the world he longed to do more than to speak to her or take her hand just once. But he had never managed to do it; he had been too shy. Since then she had been sent to a boarding school and he could hardly remember now what she looked like. Though these childish episodes seemed to come back to his mind from the remote past, they were more vivid and still possessed a more strangely nostalgic fragrance than anything else that had occurred since. They were the days when he had sat under the gateway in the evening with Naschold's Liese, peeled potatoes and listened to her stories, when he had gone very early on Sunday with his trousers turned up and a bad conscience to look for crayfish below the weir or had visited the fish trap only to get a beating from his father afterwards in his dripping Sunday suit. There had been so many puzzling and strange things and people in those days. The cobbler with his stiff neck, Strohmeyer who, as everyone knew, had poisoned his wife and the enterprising "Herr Beck" who strode all round the district with stick and knapsack and whom they all addressed as "Herr" because he had once been a rich man and had owned four horses and a carriage. Hans' knowledge of these people did not extend beyond their names and he was conscious of a feeling deep down within him that this small local world had passed him by and that there had been nothing vigorous or worthwhile to take its place.

As he had leave of absence also for the following day, he slept well into the morning, thoroughly relishing his freedom. At midday he met his father who was still agog with all his Stuttgart experiences.

" If you have passed, there may be something you'd like for yourself ? " he said good-humouredly. " Think about it ! "

"No, no," sighed the boy, "I'm quite sure I have failed."

" Silly idiot, what's come over you ? Say what you would like before I change my mind ! "

" I'd like to go fishing again in the holidays. May I ? "

" Right; you may — provided you've passed your examination."

Next day, a Sunday, there was a thunderstorm followed by a downpour of rain and Hans sat for hours reading and brooding in his room. He went over his Stuttgart performance again in great detail and came to the conclusion that he had had confounded bad luck and could have put up a far better performance. In any case he had no hope of passing. Then this idiotic headache ! He felt overcome by an increasing sense of panic and finally he went to his father in a profound state of anxiety.

" I say, father."

" What do you want ? "

" To ask something. About the wish. I would rather drop this question of fishing."

" Oh, why do you bring that up again ? "

" Because I . . . I wondered whether I might not . . ."

" Come on, out with it, what's all this tomfoolery ? What then ? "

" Go to the Grammar school if I fail."

Herr Giebenrath was speechless.

" What ? Grammar school ! " he burst out. " You at a Grammar school ! Who put that idea into your head ? "

" Nobody. It's just my own."

Deathly fear could be read on the boy's face but his father did not notice it.

" Go along," he said, forcing a laugh. " What exaggerated notions; you seem to think that I am a member of the Chamber of Commerce."

He waved the matter aside with such vigour that Hans gave up and left the room in despair.

" What a boy for you," he grumbled after him. " Well, now he wants to go to the Grammar school. Good luck to you; you're making a mistake there."

Hans sat on the window-ledge for half an hour, staring at the freshly scrubbed floorboards, and tried to imagine what it would be like if he abandoned theological college, Grammar school and study altogether. They would apprentice him to a grocer or put him in an office and he would become one of the usual run of poor people whom he despised and wanted to outshine. His handsome, intelligent schoolboy face was distorted in a grimace of pained anger; he leapt up in a rage, spat and seized the Latin anthology that lay there and flung the book with all his might against the nearest wall. Then he dashed out into the rain.

He returned to school on the Monday morning.

" How are you ? " asked the Headmaster, proffering his hand. " I thought you would come and see me yester-day. How did you fare in the examination ? "

Hans lowered his head.

" Come now ! Didn't you get on well ? "

" No; I'm afraid not."

" Come, come, patience !" The old man tried to comfort him.

" The report will probably be along from Stuttgart this morning."

The morning seemed horribly drawn out. No report arrived and Hans could hardly swallow down his dinner for anxiety.

When he entered the classroom at two in the afternoon, the form-master was already there.

" Hans Giebenrath," he shouted out loud.

Hans came forward. The master held out his hand.

" I congratulate you, Giebenrath. You have come second in the *Landexamen*."

A solemn silence ensued. The door opened and in walked the Headmaster.

" My congratulations. Now what do you say ? "

The boy was struck dumb with surprise and joy.

" Well, you don't seem to have anything to say ! "

" If I had only known that," he blurted out, " I could have come first."

" Now go along home," said the Headmaster, " and tell your father. You don't need to come back to school any more—in any case the holidays begin in a week."

The boy walked homeward down the street, his mind in a daze; he saw the lime-trees and the Market-place bathed in the sunshine — everything as before but now looking more attractive, more significant and altogether gayer. He had got through. And he had come second ! His initial joy was succeeded by a profound relief. He had no further need to avoid the Vicar. He could now get on with his studying. He could dismiss his fears about the grocer's shop and the office !

And he could take up his fishing again. His father was standing in the porch when he arrived home.

" What's the matter ? " he asked cheerfully.

" Nothing much. They've sent me home from school."

" What ? Why then ? "

" Because I'm a theological student now."

" Well, I'll be damned ! So you've got through."

Hans nodded.

" Done well ? "

" I came second."

31

The old man had not expected that. He hardly knew what to say. He kept slapping his son on the back, laughed and shook his head. Then he opened his mouth to say something. But nothing came out and he just went on shaking his head.

" Glory be ! " he finally brought out. " Glory be ! "

Hans rushed into the house, upstairs and into the loft, tore open a cupboard in the empty room, rummaged around and pulled out all sorts of boxes and bundles of lines and cork floats; his fishing tackle. The important thing now was to go out and cut a good rod. He went downstairs to his father.

" Lend me your penknife, Papa."

" What for ? "

" I must go and cut a fishing-rod."

" There," he said, beaming magnanimously, " are two Marks. You can buy a knife for yourself. But don't go to Hanfried's; go to the cutler's."

It was all done at top speed. The cutler asked about the examination, was given the good news and produced an extra handsome knife. Upstream, below the Brühelbrücke stood some fine, slender alder and hazel wands and there he cut himself a perfect, strong but springy rod and hurried back home with it.

His face flushed and his eyes gleaming he set about the cheerful task of preparing his tackle, a thing he enjoyed almost as much as the actual fishing. He sat over it all afternoon and evening. The white, brown and green lines were sorted out, carefully inspected, repaired and freed of many old knots and tangles. Cork floats and quills of all shapes and sizes were tested or freshly cut; small leaden shot of various weights were hammered into sinkers and provided with notches for weighting the lines. Next was the turn of the hooks of which he still had a small supply. These he fastened partly on four-ply black thread, partly on twisted horsehair. Towards evening it was all ready and Hans knew that he would have no hours of boredom before him in the long, seven-week holiday, for once he had his fishing rod he could spend whole days alone by the river.

CHAPTER TWO

It was how summer holidays ought to be. Gentian-blue skies above the hills, one blazing hot day after another for weeks on end, only occasionally interrupted by a short thunderstorm. The river, despite the fact that it flowed between many sandstone cliffs and narrow gorges, often overshadowed by pine forests, was so warm that it was possible to bathe right up to late evening. The scent of hay from the second crop hung all round the small town; the narrow strips of the few cornfields were turning russet and gold; along by the streams hemlock with its white flowers and giant umbels, permanently covered with tiny insects and its hollow stems that can be made into primitive flutes and pipes had grown man-high. Long, stately rows of downy leafed yellow mullein shone at the edges of the wood; greater and rose-bay willow herb swayed on their long, slender stalks, the latter transforming whole hillsides into a sea of purple. Under the shade of the pine-trees the tall foxglove with its broad silvery root-leaves, its strong, rigid stem and closely set red flowers stood there, looking staid, handsome, rather exotic. Close by were various kinds of fungi—the red, shiny fly-agaric, the broad fleshy mushroom, the adventurous Bear's Paw fungus, the knobbly coral-mushroom and the odd, colourless, sickly-looking Pine Bird's Nest. On the many heather-covered ridges between the woods and meadows blazed tough, yellow broom, then came strips of purple heather, followed by the fields most of them still waiting for the second mowing, a many-coloured profusion of Lady's

Smock, campion, sage, and scabious. The woods were filled with the unending song of the chaffinches, red squirrels in the pine-forest ran over the tree-tops, green lizards gleamed and panted happily on ridges, walls and in dry ditches and over the meadows sounded the untiring, high-pitched chirrup of the cicadas.

The town was particularly bucolic at this time of the year with the hay-carts, the smell of hay, and the ring of the scythes on the whetting-stones filling the streets and the air around; but for the two factories you might have been in a village.

Early on the morning of the first day of his holiday, Hans was already standing impatiently in the kitchen waiting for his coffee almost as soon as old Anna was down. He helped to make the fire, fetched bread from the breadbowl, rushed down with the coffee cooled with fresh milk, crammed some bread into his pockets and ran off. He stopped at the top railway embankment, drew a cylindrical tin box out of his trouser pocket and set about the job of catching grasshoppers. The trains passed by but not at speed because of the steep gradient at that spot; they chuffed along at a nice comfortable pace with all the windows open and perhaps a handful of passengers, allowing a long cheerful plume of smoke and steam to trail behind it. He watched it go by and observed how the whitish smoke curled up but was soon lost in the clear early-morning air. How long it had been since he had seen it! He heaved great sighs as if he was eager to catch up on the gay months he had missed with all possible haste and become once more a small, completely ordinary and irresponsible schoolboy. His heart beat with secret delight and in anticipation of the catch as he strode over the bridge and behind, through the gardens to the *Gaulsgumpen*, the deepest spot in the river, with his tin of grass-hoppers and his new rod. He knew a corner where, leaning against a willow-trunk, one could fish in greater comfort and with less disturbance than anywhere else. He unwound the line, fitted on a small lead shot, ruthlessly impaled a fat grasshopper on the hook and cast the line with a wide swing towards the middle of the river. The old familiar game began; the small bleak swarmed round his bait and tried to pull it off the hook. Before long it was nibbled off; a second grasshopper replaced the first then another and fourth and a fifth. He fixed them to the hook with increasing care; finally he weighted the line with an additional shot and now the first sizeable fish went for the bait. It nibbled at it for a second or two, let it go again, then tried once more.

Now it bit properly—a good fisherman feels the tug along his line and rod right into his fingers. Hans gave an adroit jerk and cautiously drew in his line. The fish sulked and as it became visible, Hans recognised a rudd. It can be immediately identified by its broad, yellowish-white shimmering body, the triangular head and beautiful flesh-pink on the ventral fins. How much did it weigh? But before he could test it, the fish gave a desperate jerk, thrashed about in a panic on the surface and got away. He could still see it as it turned three or four times in the water and then disappeared into the depths like a flash of silver lightning. It had not been properly hooked.

The excitement and intense concentration of the sport was now awakened in our angler. He kept his eye on the thin brown line where it broke the surface, his cheeks were flushed, his movements, short, swift and sure. A second rudd bit and was landed, then a small carp that he felt almost ashamed not to throw back, then three gudgeon in succession. He was specially pleased about the gudgeon to which his father was particularly partial. They have thick bodies covered with tiny scales, a fat head with a comic white beard, small eyes and a slender abdomen. Their colour is half-way between green and brown which shades into steel-blue when it is landed.

The sun had climbed high by now, the foam on the upper weir shone as white as snow; the warm air shimmered above the water and when he looked up he could see a few small dazzlingly white clouds poised above the Muckberg. It was growing hot. Nothing expresses the heat of an untroubled midsummer day better than a few peaceful clouds suspended peaceful and white, midway as it were in the blue sky and so saturated with light that you cannot bear to look at them long. But for them you would often be unaware how hot it is; it is not when you see the blue sky nor the glittering river surface but when you catch sight of these few compact, foam-white mid-day sailors that you suddenly become conscious of the sun's heat, seek out the shade and pass your hands over your damp forehead.

Hans gradually paid less and less attention to his angling. He was rather tired and in any case one rarely catches anything much about noon. The carp, even the oldest and largest, surface to sun themselves. They swim dreamily upstream close to the surface in big dark shoals, sometimes take fright without visible cause and refuse to bite during this period of time.

Hans cast his line into the water over a willow branch, sat down on the grass and gazed at the green water. The fish slowly rose; one dark back after another appeared on the surface—quiet, slowly swimming in magic shoals, drawn irresistibly upwards by the heat. They must feel marvellous in the warm water ! Hans pulled off his shoes and allowed his feet to dangle in the water which was quite tepid on the surface. He inspected his catch; the fish were swimming round in a large bucket with an occasional soft swish. How handsome they were ! White, brown, green, silver, dull gold, blue and other colours gleamed at every movement of their scales and fins.

It was very quiet. You could hardly hear the rumble of the carts as they crossed the bridge and the splash of the mill-wheel was barely audible from where he was standing. The only real sound was the gentle unending rush of the cool white water as it poured lazily over the weir and swirled softly past the floating timbers of the rafts.

Greek and Latin grammar and composition, arithmetic and " rep " and the whole torturing turmoil of a long, restless and hectic year sank quietly away from him in the warm, drowsy hour. He had a slight headache but it was not as bad as before and he could now sit by the water's edge again; he watched the foam breaking into spray dust by the weir, blinked at his line, conscious of the fish closer at hand, swimming in the bucket. It was wonderful and meantime he had remembered that he had passed the *Landexamen* and had won the second place, and he splashed his naked feet in the water, thrust both hands into his trouser pockets and began to whistle a tune. He could not really whistle; it had been a sore point in the old days and he had been ragged about it a good deal by his school-fellows. He could only whistle through his teeth and even then only very softly, but it was good enough for home purposes; at all events no one could hear him at the present moment. The others were in school, having a geography lesson; he alone was free and out of it. He had outstripped them and they were now below him. They had tormented him enough; apart from August he had had no friends and had taken no pleasure in their games and fights. Well, they could watch him now, the dolts. He despised them so much that he stopped whistling for a moment to make a grimace. Then he wound in his line and could not help laughing for there was no bait left on the hook. He released the grasshoppers left in the tin and they crawled dazed and disconsolately into the short grass. Not far away was the tannery; they had broken off for dinner; it was time he went off for his.

Hardly a word was said at table.

" Caught anything ? " asked his father.

" Five."

" Have you ? Well, mind you don't catch the old'un or there won't be any little fish later on."

After that the conversation lapsed. It was so hot. It was such a shame, too, that you were not allowed to bathe straight after a meal. Why was it ? It was supposed to be harmful ! But was there any harm in it ? Hans knew better; despite the ban he had gone bathing often enough. But never again; he was too grown up for such larks. Heavens above, they had addressed him as " Mr." at the examination.

Anyhow he would not mind enjoying an hour lying in the garden under the spruce-tree. There was plenty of shade and one could either read or watch butterflies. He lay there until two o'clock in the afternoon and very nearly went off to sleep. Now for a swim ! Only a few boys were at the bathing spot, all the older ones were in school, and Hans felt genuinely sorry for them. He slowly slipped off his clothes and lowered himself into the water. He knew all about enjoying warmth followed by coolness and vice-versa; first he swam about for a while, did some diving and splashing round; then he lay prostrate on the bank and felt the sun's heat on his quickly drying skin. The younger boys crept round him in awe. Yes; he had become a celebrity. In point of fact he looked very different from the rest of them. The sensitive head with the intelligent face and thoughtful eyes sat easily and attractively on the narrow, bronzed neck. And he was slender-limbed and delicate looking; you could count his ribs, and he had practically no calves.

He was in and out of the water almost the whole afternoon. After four o'clock most of the members of his own class came shouting up.

" Hello, Giebenrath! You're all right! "

He stretched himself luxuriously. " Yes I'm all right! "

" When do you go to the theological college? "

" Not till September. It's the vacation now."

He let them envy him. He did not even worry when the jeering in the background grew loud and one of them sang:

> " If only my life could be like
> Schulze's Lisabeth!
> She lies all day in bed.
> No such luck for me."

Hans merely laughed. Meantime the boys undressed. One leaped straight into the water; others, more cautious, cooled down first and a number of them lay down in the grass for a while. One who was a good diver won the general admiration. A nervous boy was pushed backwards into the river and called out " Murder! " They chased each other, ran, swam, splashed the dry ones on the bank. The noise of splashing and shrieking was terrific and the whole breadth of the river gleamed with wet, glistening bodies.

Hans went off an hour later. The warm evening hours

descended—the period when the fish begin to bite again. He fished from the bridge until supper. The fish were greedy, the bait was snapped up every minute but he did not manage to hook anything. He was using cherries for bait; evidently they were too soft. He decided to try again later.

They told him at supper-time that a crowd of acquaintances had called to congratulate him. And they showed him the current weekly paper in which under the heading " Official News " was the following notice:

" This year our town sent only one candidate in for the Entrance Examination of the Junior Theological College, Hans Giebenrath. We are pleased to learn that the said candidate has won the second place."

He folded the paper, put it in his pocket and said nothing but he was filled with pride and joy. Then he returned to his fishing. This time he took a few crumbs of cheese along with him for bait; the fish like it and it can easily be seen by them in the dusk.

He left his rod behind, contenting himself with a line. He preferred fishing without a rod and without having to hold the float in his hand—so that his sole tackle consisted merely of a line and hook. It was rather more laborious but pleasanter. You could control the slightest movement of the bait, feel every nibble and bite and follow the movements of the fish jerking the line as if you could actually see them in front of you. Naturally this method of fishing has to be properly understood and you need clever fingers and all the alertness of a spy.

Twilight fell early in the narrow, deeply cut and winding valley. The water lay black and tranquil under the bridge; there was already a light in the lower mill. Chatter and song could be heard on the bridges and in the narrow streets; it was rather sultry, and every minute a dark fish would give a short leap into the air. Fish become remarkably excitable on such evenings; they dart hither and thither, jump out of the water, hit against the line and hurl themselves blindly on to the bait. By time the last fragment of cheese was used up, Hans had pulled out four smaller carp and he intended to take them to the vicar the next day.

A warm breeze swept down the valley. It got very dark but the sky was still light. Only the church tower and castle roof rose black and sharply into the clear sky from the darkening town below. There must have been a thunderstorm somewhere in the remote distance; you could still hear an occasional faint rumble.

When Hans climbed into bed at ten o'clock, he was agreeably tired in head and limb in a way he had not experienced for some time. A long series of lovely summer days stretched out before him, peaceful and alluring, days for idling, bathing, fishing, day-dreaming. Only one thing worried him; he had not come first in the examination.

By early noon he was already standing under the ogee arch of the vicarage, delivering his fish. The vicar emerged from his study.

" Oh, Hans Giebenrath! Good morning! Allow me to congratulate you most heartily. And what have you got there ? "

" Just a few fish. I went fishing yesterday."

" Well, look here ! Thank you very much. But do come in."

Hans entered the already familiar study. It did not look like the average parson's study. It smelt neither of plants nor tobacco. The considerable library displayed almost nothing but new, freshly varnished and gilded book covers, none of the mouldy, worm-eaten volumes with broken spines that you normally encounter in vicarage libraries. A closer inspection revealed the presence of a new spirit, one that was certainly very different from that associated with the fast disappearing generation of respectable, old-fashioned gentlemen. The highly-esteemed show-pieces of a parson's library, the volumes by Bengel, Oetinger and Steinhofer and the mystical hymn-writers whom Mörike treats so affectionately in his *Turmhahn* were lacking here or submerged among a host of modern works. Everything in short from the periodical-holder, lectern and large desk strewn with papers looked serious and learned. You got the impression that a great deal of work went on here, as indeed it did: not so much in the way of sermons, catechisms and bible-readings as research and articles for learned periodicals and preliminary study for his own books. Inner searchings, vague mysticism had no place there any more than the ingenuous and intuitive brand of theology which bridges the golf of knowledge and responds to the emotional needs of the thirsty souls of the common folk. Instead, Bible criticism and the search for the " Historical Christ " was carried out with zeal.

Theology is no different from any other subject; there is the theology which is art and the other which is science at any rate trying to be science. This was as true yesterday as it is now; scientific scholars have always neglected the old wine for the new bottles whereas those with the aesthetic approach, persisting regardlessly in many apparent heresies have brought joy and comfort to many. It is the old unequal struggle between criticism and creation, knowledge and art; and while representatives of the former may have been invariably right, without gain to anybody, the latter continued to scatter the seeds of belief, love, comfort, and beauty and a feeling of eternity and were for ever discovering good ground. For life is stronger than death and belief more powerful than doubt.

For the first time in his life Hans sat down on the small hide sofa between the lectern and the window. The vicar was in a particularly amiable mood. He talked about the Theological College in a friendly fashion, describing how one lived and studied there.

"The most important new thing," he concluded, "will be your introduction to New Testament Greek. It will open up a fresh world to you, rich in work and pleasure. The language will present difficulties at first; it isn't Attic Greek but a new Greek, that is an idiom that was called into being by a new spirit."

Hans listened eagerly, proud to feel that real knowledge was now within his grasp.

"The academic introduction to this new world," continued the vicar, "detracts a good deal from its magic. At College Hebrew will at first make perhaps too exclusive a claim on your attention. If you like we could make a modest start during the present holidays. You will be glad to have some time and superfluous energy for other things in the College. We could begin with a few chapters of Luke together and you would learn the language at the same time, almost like a game. I can lend you a dictionary. You could devote one hour—or two at the most—a day to it. Not more. Naturally the all-important thing is for you to have the period of relaxation you have earned. It's only a suggestion of course. I wouldn't like to spoil your feeling of holiday."

Hans naturally fell in with the plan. Although the St. Luke lesson loomed like a small cloud in the cheerful blue sky of his freedom, he was ashamed to decline the offer.

Furthermore the idea of learning a new language in the holidays seemed more in the nature of pleasure than a task. And he was slightly nervous about the host of new subjects he would have to tackle in the Theological College, especially Hebrew.

So he was by no means downcast when he left the vicar and he made his way up through the avenue of larches to the forest. The slight misgivings he had felt had already vanished and the more he thought the matter over, the more acceptable it seemed to him, for he was well aware that he would have to apply himself to his work with even more ardour in the training college if he intended to outstrip his fellow students. And that certainly was his aim. But why? He was not even sure himself. For three years, now, they had all kept their eyes fastened on him—teachers, the vicar, his father and the Headmaster had urged him on and had never given him a moment's rest. The whole time, from one class to the next, he had been indisputably first. And now it had gradually become a point of honour with him to remain top and brook no rival. But the stupid examination was over.

Holidays were undoubtedly the best time. How unusually beautiful the forest looked these morning hours when there was no one else there except himself. The pine trunks stood in serried rows like pillars in a vast hall vaulted with a blue-green roof. There was little undergrowth—only a wild raspberry bush here and there—instead, a mile-wide, soft, fungus-covered and mossy floor on which low bilberry plants and heather also grew. The dew had already evaporated and the characteristic morning closeness compounded of the sun's heat and a smell of mist, moss, resin, pine-needles and fungi, assailed the senses with a faint but irresistible intoxication. Hans flung himself down on the moss, collected and ate bilberries from the dense plants, heard a green woodpecker hammering away at a tree-trunk and listened to the calls of a jealous cuckoo. The sky showed a deep, cloudless blue through the dark pine-tops and the thousands of perpendicular trunks closed in to form an impressive brown wall, and here and there a patch of sunlight fell warm and gleaming on to the mossy ground.

Hans had originally intended to go for a long walk, at least as far as the Lützeler Farm or the crocus-meadow. But there he was lying on the moss, eating bilberries and idly gazing into the sky full of wonder. He began to feel surprised at feeling so tired. In the old days a three or four hours' walk had been a mere nothing. He resolved to shake off his torpor and have a good walk and he stepped out for a few hundred yards. Then somehow he found himself lying down on the mossy ground again. There he lay, letting his dazzled eyes rove among the tree-tops, in and among the trunks and over the green earth. How relaxed this air made him feel!

When he went back home about mid-day, he had a headache again. His eyes hurt him too; the sun had been beating down so mercilessly on the forest path. He sat about indoors during the afternoon, frustrated and did not feel refreshed until he had a bathe. By then it was time to go to the vicar's.

Flaig, the shoemaker, who was sitting on his three-legged stool, caught sight of him as he went past and invited him in.

" Where are you off, son ? We never see anything of you these days."

" I must go to the vicar's now."

" Still ? But the examination's over."

46

" Yes. It's something else now. New Testament. That is the New Testament in Greek; but it's quite a different Greek from the Greek I have learned. I've got to learn that now."

The shoemaker pushed his hat back and screwed his large, meditative brow into deep furrows. He gave a deep sigh.

" Hans," he said in a gentle voice, " I will tell you something. I've kept my mouth shut so far because of the examination but now I must warn you. The vicar is a sceptic. He will state and try and prove that the Holy scriptures are false, and if you read the New Testament with him you will lose your own faith without knowing why."

" But, Herr Flaig, it is merely a question of Greek. In any case I shall have to learn it at the Theological college."

" That's what you say, but it's quite a different matter doing the Bible with learned and pious teachers from doing it with someone who has ceased to believe in God."

" Yes, but we don't know whether he really has stopped believing."

" We do, Hans. Unfortunately."

" What am I to do then ? I have already agreed to go to him."

" Then obviously you must. But if he should refer to the Bible as being the work of men and therefore false and not inspired by the Holy Spirit, you must come to me and we will have a talk about it. Do you agree ? "

" Yes, Herr Flaig. But it won't come to that."

" You wait. Don't forget about coming to me."

The vicar was out and Hans had to wait for him in the study. As he inspected the gilt-lettered book-titles, the shoemaker's words came back into his mind. He had often heard similar views expressed about the vicar and in particular about the new-style priest but now, for the first time he felt caught up and intensely interested in a personal way. They did not assume for him the scandalous importance with which the shoemaker regarded them; he guessed that old beliefs still lay hidden behind them. In his earlier schooldays, the questions of God's continual presence, the seat of human souls, devil and hell, had sometimes aroused fantastic speculations in his mind, but during the last strenuous and trying years all these questions had slumbered and his schoolboy Christian belief was only occasionally brought into the realm of his personal life when he engaged in discussions with the vicar. He could not help smiling when he compared the latter with Flaig. The boy could not understand the shoemaker's rigid attitude which had been acquired in the course of years of embittered determination, and if Flaig was intelligent, he was also ingenuous and prejudiced and ridiculed by many for his exaggerated piety. He was stern, uncompromising in laying down the law and a formidable evangelist at the meetings of the Brotherhood; he also ran instruction classes in the neighbouring villages. In other respects, however, he was merely an artisan and no less limited in outlook than the rest of them. The vicar, on the other hand, was not only intellectual and an eloquent preacher but a hard-working and stern scholar. Hans gazed with awe at his rows of books.

The vicar soon arrived. He exchanged his outdoor coat for a black light-weight jacket, handed the boy the Greek text of St. Luke and asked him to read. It was very different from the Latin lessons. They read only a few sentences which were then translated with laborious literalness and then taking most unpromising examples, the vicar expatiated on the spirit of the language with much eloquence and persuasion; he went on to speak about the origins of the Book and in this single lesson introduced the boy to an entirely new conception of learning and reading. Hans thus obtained some idea of the problems and tasks that lay concealed in each verse and word and how thousands of scholars, inquirers and philosophers had puzzled over these questions since the earliest times, and he realized that even he himself in the present lesson was being caught up in the circle of seekers after truth.

He was lent a lexicon and a grammar, and worked away at home the whole evening. It now became clear to him over what mountains of work and knowledge the path to true scholarship would lead him, and he was ready to follow it without tarrying by the wayside. For the time being the shoemaker was forgotten.

This new life completely absorbed him for some days. Every afternoon he went to the vicar's and every day real erudition seemed a finer, more difficult and more worthwhile object. He went fishing in the early morning hours and each afternoon found him at the bathing meadow; apart from that he scarcely left the house. His ambition, previously submerged in the anxiety and triumph of the examination, was now awake again and gave him no rest. But at the same time he was suffering from a recurrence of the peculiar sensation in his head which he had felt so often during the last months — not pain but a restless quickening of his pulse, an excited energy, a terrific urge to drive himself on. The headache came afterwards but while the fever lasted his reading and work in general proceeded at a furious rate, and he would read the most difficult sentences in Xenophon, each one of which would normally have taken him a quarter of an hour, with almost comic ease. At such periods he hardly needed the lexicon and his alert brain was able to tackle difficult whole pages cheerfully and quickly. This feverish activity and thirst for recognition was accompanied by a certain feeling of pride on his part, as if the world of school and teachers and years of study lay far behind him and he was already treading his own path towards the peaks of knowledge and learning.

He was feeling like that just now and his sleep was restless and frequently interrupted by strangely clear dreams. When he woke up in the night suffering from a slight headache and was unable to get off to sleep again, this impatience to get on was mixed with pride as he thought how far ahead he was of all his school-friends and how teachers and the Headmaster had regarded him with a kind of respect akin to admiration.

The latter derived an inward satisfaction from guiding the laudible ambition he had aroused in his pupil and from watching it grow. Let it never be said that schoolmasters have no heart and that they are soulless and fossilized pedants ! Far from it; when a teacher sees a child's long dormant talent bursting out, sees a boy laying aside his wooden sword, sling and bow and arrow and other childish toys, sees him beginning to strive forward, sees serious work transforming a rough chubby face into one that is refined, almost ascetic, watches this face as it becomes more intellectual, the glance deeper and more purposeful, his hands whiter and less fidgety, then it is that his soul laughs within him, full of joy and pride. His duty, the task with which the State has entrusted him requires that he shall subdue and extirpate untutored energy and natural appetites and plant in their place the quiet, temperate ideals recognised by the State. Many a person who is at present a contented citizen and persevering official might have become an undisciplined innovator or futile dreamer but for these efforts on the part of the school. There was something wild, untamed, uncultured in him that must first be broken, a dangerous flame that must be extinguished and stamped out. Man as Nature created him is a dark, incalculable and dangerous creature—a spring that bursts forth from an unknown mountain, an ancient forest without path or clearing. An ancient forest must be cleared and tidied up and greatly reduced in area; it is the school's job to break in the natural man, subdue and greatly reduce him; in accordance with principles sanctioned by authority it is its task to make him a useful member of the community and awake in him those qualities, the complete development of which is brought to a triumphant conclusion by the well-calculated discipline of the barrack square.

How well young Giebenrath had developed. He had almost entirely given up games and generally idling about on his own accord; his stupid giggling in class was a thing of the past; he had even abandoned gardening, rabbit-keeping and the wretched sport of fishing.

One evening the Headmaster appeared at the Giebenrath house in person. After he had politely dismissed the flattered father he went into Hans' room where he found the boy sitting over St. Luke's Gospel. He greeted him in the most cheerful manner.

" Splendid Giebenrath, busy again already ! But why don't you show yourself any more ? I keep expecting you every day."

" I would have come before," Hans said, excusing himself, " but I wanted to have a nice fish to bring you."

" Fish, what sort of a fish ? "

" Oh, a carp or something of that kind."

" You're fishing again, then ? "

" Yes, to some extent. Father's given me permission."

" Do you enjoy it much ? "

" Rather ! "

" Very nice too. You've certainly earned your holidays. I don't suppose you are very anxious to do any work as well ? "

" Oh yes, I am."

" Mind you I should hate to feel I'm forcing anything on you that you don't want to do yourself."

" But I *do* want to."

The Headmaster drew a few deep breaths, stroked his thin beard and sat down on a chair.

" Look here Hans, it's like this. Past experience goes to show that a very good examination result is often followed by a sudden reaction. You will have to tackle several new subjects at the Theological College. There are always a number of boys who have been preparing work during the holidays—in fact it's often just the ones who haven't distinguished themselves particularly in the examination. They suddenly leap ahead of those who have rested on their laurels during the vacation."

He gave another sigh.

" Here at school you've never had any difficulty in maintaining your position at the head of the form. But at college you'll find other boys just as talented or very hard-working who won't be outstripped so easily. Do you see my point ? "

" Why yes."

" Now, I propose that you should do a little preliminary work during the holidays. Not too much of course ! You have the right and duty to yourself to take a good rest. I thought one hour—or perhaps two a day would be about the right amount. Otherwise it is easy to get rusty and then it takes weeks to get going again. What do you think ? "

" I am quite ready, Sir, if it doesn't mean too much trouble for you."

" Good. Next to Hebrew, Homer will open up a new world to you. You would read him with redoubled pleasure and understanding later if we could lay a solid foundation now. Homer's tongue, the old Ionian dialect, and Homeric prosody are somewhat peculiar—it constitutes a language of its own and requires hard work and a sound basis if one is to come to a full appreciation of the poetry."

Hans was, of course, quite prepared to penetrate the said world and promised to do his best. The thick end of the wedge was to come. The Headmaster cleared his throat and continued in the same amiable tone.

" It would also please me if you would agree to devote a few hours to mathematics. You're not a bad arithmetician but so far maths has hardly been your strong point. At the Theological College you will have to do Algebra and Geometry and you would be well advised to have a few preliminary lessons."

" I agree."

" You are always welcome at my house, you know that. It's a point of honour with me to see vou achieve great things. As far as the maths are concerned, you must ask your father to let you take some private tuition with the mathematics master. Possibly three or four a week."

" Certainly, sir."

Work was now in full swing again and if Hans fished or had a walk for the occasional odd hour, he felt a bad conscience. He had had to sacrifice his usual bathing period for his lessons with the mathematics master.

Work at them as he did, Hans was unable to derive any pleasure from his algebra lessons. It was grim indeed on a hot afternoon to have to go to the master's stuffy room instead of the bathing meadow and repeat $a+b$ and $a-b$ when his brain was tired and his throat parched in the dusty, midge-filled air. A heavy and oppressive atmosphere hung over him which on bad days easily turned into depression and despair. He did not make spectacular progress with his mathematics but he was not on the other hand one of those pupils to whom the subject is impossible; sometimes he found good and even neat solutions and felt pleased. What he liked about mathematics was that it did not allow of any fallacy or possibility of deviation from the matter in hand or trespassing on adjacent but alien territory.

He found Latin attractive for the same reason, namely that it is clear, certain, unequivocal and ambiguity is almost unknown. But in mathematics even when all the results tallied nothing particularly right emerged. Books and lessons to do with the subject were like walking along a flat country road; you moved forward, every day you grasped something you had failed to understand the previous day but you never reached mountain heights from which you all at once discovered extensive views.

The lessons with the Headmaster were becoming more stimulating. It was true that the vicar always managed to make something more attractive and impressive out of the degenerate Old Testament Greek than the former out of Homer's language with all its youthful freshness. But it

54

was really Homer that surprised, delighted, lured you on, once you had overcome the initial difficulties. Hans often sat full of trembling impatience and excitement before a cryptic, melodious but difficult line, in his eagerness to find the key which would open up the gay, tranquil garden.

He now had any amount of homework again and on many occasions he sat at the table deeply absorbed in some task until late into the night. Herr Giebenrath noticed this industry with some pride. There vaguely existed in his dull head the ideal cherished by so many people of limited intelligence; he imagined a branch stemming from himself and reaching above him to a height which he could only gaze at in silent awe.

The Headmaster and the vicar suddenly became noticeably more indulgent and considerate for the last weeks of his holidays. They sent the boy for walks, discontinued their lessons and emphasized how important it was for him to embark on the new stage in his career alert and refreshed.

Hans went fishing a few times. He was suffering from frequent headaches and would sit rather absent-mindedly by the banks of the river which now reflected a pale blue autumn sky. He was puzzled as to why he should have so looked forward to the summer holidays. At present he was glad that they were over and that he was on the point of entering a college where an entirely different programme of life and work would begin. As he had by now become somewhat indifferent to his fishing he practically never caught a fish, and on one occasion when his father teased him on the subject he put his lines away in the tin box in the attic.

Only in the last few days did it suddenly occur to him that he had not been to the shoemaker Flaig for weeks.

Even then he had to force himself to call. It was evening and Flaig was sitting by his parlour window with a small child on each knee. The smell of leather and blacking permeated the whole house despite the open window. Feeling embarrassed Hans put his hand in the shoemaker's broad palm.

"Well, how's it going?" he asked. "Have you worked hard for the vicar?"

"Yes; I've been along every day and learned a good deal."

"What sort of things?"

"Greek mainly but other things too."

"And you never felt the urge to come to me?"

"Felt it certainly, Herr Flaig, but I could never manage it. A lesson with the vicar every day and two a day with the Headmaster and then I had to go to the Maths master four times a week."

"What now, during the holidays? It's senseless!"

"I don't know. The masters wanted me to and I find studying comes fairly easily to me."

"That may be," said Flaig, gripping the boy's arm.

"It wouldn't matter about the learning but look at those thin arms of yours and your face is so thin. Do you still get headaches?"

"Now and again."

"It is all wrong and a sin. At your age you should have air and exercise and the proper amount of rest. What are the holidays for? Certainly not for sitting indoors and more study. You are nothing but skin and bone."

Hans laughed.

"Oh yes, you will win through. But too much is too much. And what about the lessons with the vicar. What had he to say?"

" Many things but nothing you would have disapproved of. He knows a terrific amount."

" And he didn't speak disrespectfully about the Bible ? "

" No; not once."

" Good. For I must say this: better ten times damage to your body than hurt to your soul ! You intend to become a clergyman later; it is a responsible and difficult office and needs a different type of candidate from most of the young men to-day. Perhaps you are the right material and will become a helper and teacher of souls. I desire that with all my heart and I will pray to that end."

He had risen to his feet and now laid both hands firmly on the boy's shoulders.

" Goodbye Hans; be a good lad ! May the Lord bless and keep you, Amen."

Hans found this solemnity, blessing and archaic language heavy and distasteful. The vicar's manner when he took leave of him had been very different.

His last few days flashed by in a fever of preparation and leave-taking. A trunk containing his bed-linen, clothes and books had already been sent off and one cool morning father and son started for Maulbronn. It was a depressing and odd experience to be leaving his native town and father's house and going to a strange establishment.

CHAPTER THREE

The large Cistercian monastery of Maulbronn lies in the north west of the Province among wooded hills and small peaceful lakes. The lovely old buildings are extensive, solid and well-preserved and would tempt anyone to live there, for they are handsome both within and without, and in the course of the centuries they have gradually become a harmonious part of their beautiful setting. The visitor to the monastery enters by a picturesque gateway in the high wall on to a wide and tranquil close. A stream runs through it; here and there, on both sides, stand ancient trees and solid stone buildings; in the background rises the façade of the main church building with a late-romanesque porch, the " Galilee," of incomparable grace and charm. A comic little tower with a slender steeple—it hardly seems credible that it can house a bell—is perched on the vast church roof. The gem of the transept, still perfectly intact and itself a fine piece of work, is an exquisite well-chapel; the monks' refectory with its noble, ribbed vaulting, oratory, parlour, lay refectory, abbot's house and two churches compose an impressive whole. Picturesque walls, bow-windows, gateways, gardens, a mill, dwelling houses form a gay and homely contrast to the dignified and ancient buildings which they encircle. The spacious close lies empty and still and plays a drowsy game with the shadows of its trees. Only in the hour following mid-day does a fleeting semblance of life pass over it, for at that time a horde of youths emerge from the monastery and scatter over the vast area to the lively accompaniment of shouts, conversation and laughter, sometimes play a ball game and then, after the recreation hour has ended, quickly disappear behind the walls without leaving a trace. There must be many who have reflected to themselves as they stood on this square that here was the place for a healthy period of life and happiness, that something alive and beneficent was bound to thrive here and that in this place if anywhere mature, good men must think their joyful thoughts and accomplish their cheerful works.

This remote and magnificent monastery, hidden away behind hills and forests has long been given over to the students of the Protestant Theological College so that these sensitive young men may live in an environment of beauty and peace. Furthermore they are in this way removed from the distracting influences of towns and family life and shielded from the harmful spectacle of mundane activity. By this means it is possible to ensure that the study of Greek and Hebrew and of other serious related subjects will loom before them for years as their life's goal and turn these thirsty young souls to pure and idealistic pursuits and pleasures. Boarding school life is an important factor in this system with its emphasis on self reliance and community spirit. The foundation at the expense of which these students are privileged to live and study has seen to it that its pupils are imbued with a special spirit by which they can be recognised later on—a refined and definite hallmark as it were. Except for the undisciplined who occasionally kick over the traces, every Swabian theological student can be recognised as such for the rest of his life.

The boys whose mothers are still living at the time when their sons enter the College remember the day with wistful gratitude. Hans Giebenrath was not one of these;

he left home without emotion but he could not help seeing a great number of other boys' mothers and it left a strange impression on him. In the so-called dormitories which were virtually long corridors lined with cupboards stood trunks and baskets, and the boys accompanied by their parents were busy unpacking their things. Each boy had a numbered locker and was shown his allotted bookshelf in the Study. Parents and sons bent over their unpacking on the floor; the student teacher wandered in their midst like a prince, occasionally offering a well-meant piece of advice. Unpacked clothes were spread out, shirts folded, books piled up, shoes and slippers set out in rows. For the majority of the boys the college outfit was more or less identical, as there was a prescribed list of the minimum articles of underclothing and other essential garments. Tin wash basins with the boys' names scratched on were put out in the wash-room together with sponge, soap-dish, comb and tooth-brush. Each boy had brought in addition a lamp, a can of paraffin and a set of table utensils.

All the boys were very pre-occupied and excited. Their fathers smilingly tried to lend a hand, kept consulting their watches between intervals of boredom, and made an effort to remain in the background. It was the mothers who were the busy ones. They picked up the various articles of clothing, smoothed the creases out of them, pulled tapes straight and separated all the different items ready for packing them neatly folded in the wardrobes. There was a steady flow of admonitions, suggestions, and affectionate encouragement accompanying all this activity.

" You must be specially careful with your new shirts; they cost three marks fifty each."

" You are to send your laundry by rail once a month—

by parcel post, if there's a hurry. You must keep your black hat for Sundays."

A fat, comfortable-looking woman sat on a large trunk, teaching her son the art of sewing on buttons.

"If you feel homesick," another was saying, "keep writing to me — it's not such a dreadful long time to Christmas."

A pretty, still fairly young mother was inspecting her son's wardrobe and passing her hand tenderly over the pile of linen, coats and trousers. When she had finished she began to caress her boy. The chubby-cheeked, broad-shouldered child was trying to stop her and gave an embarrassed laugh; so as not to seem a milksop he thrust both hands into his trouser-pockets. The leave-taking appeared to affect him less than his mother.

Conversely with some of the others. They gazed helplessly at their preoccupied mothers and looked as though they would much prefer to go back home with them. A great struggle was going on in all their breasts—apprehension at being left and the heightened feeling of affection and dependency on the one hand versus shyness before the other boys and the defiant self-assertion of adolescence on the other. A number of the boys who were really on the point of tears assumed an expression of casual indifference and behaved as though they were not particularly concerned and the mothers too put on smiles. Almost every boy had some "extras" over and above prescribed items to unpack from his trunk — they included among other things sacks of apples, smoked sausages and baskets of pastry. A number of them had brought their skates. One diminutive, sly-looking boy was attracting considerable attention through the possession of a whole ham which he took no pains to hide.

It was not difficult to sort out those who came straight from home from those who had already been in other boarding schools or similar establishments. But even among the latter a certain excitement and tension could be detected.

Herr Giebenrath was helping his son with the unpacking and he set about it in a deft and practical manner. He had finished before most of the others and was standing beside Hans in the dormitory looking bored. As he noticed fathers on all sides admonishing and moralizing, mothers handing out comfort and good advice and their dazed sons listening, he thought it fitting that he should start his Hans off on the path of life with some golden words of his own. He cogitated for some minutes and then sidled up to his son in a rather embarrassed manner and suddenly opened fire with a selection of hackneyed injunctions which Hans listened to in dumb amazement until he caught sight of a pastor standing there smiling at his father's speeches. He was overcome with shame and drew the speaker over towards him.

" Well, I trust you will be a credit to your family and obey the authorities ? "

" Yes, of course," said Hans.

His father stopped and heaved a sigh of relief. He was beginning to get bored with it all. Hans too felt somewhat bewildered—one minute he was looking in dazed curiosity through the window and down into the quiet cloister with its age-old peace and dignity which contrasted so strangely with the boisterous young life above—the next, glancing nervously at his busy fellow pupils not one of whom he knew so far. His acquaintance from the Stuttgart Land-examen did not appear to have gained admittance for all his superior Göppinger Latin—at any rate Hans could not see him anywhere. Without giving the matter much thought, he ran his eye over his future companions. Though their clothes were so similar in style and composed of more or less the same items, he found no difficulty in distinguishing the townees from the farmers' sons, the rich from the poor. Sons of wealthy parents did not often come to the College in point of fact, attendance at which was partly determined by the parents' pride or foresight; all the same, a number of professors and higher officials continued to send their sons to Maulbronn in memory of their own years in the monastery. Thus a wide variety of cloths and cuts was to be seen among the forty black coats present and even more marked were the differences in manners, dialects and bearing among the young people themselves. They included lithe, strong-limbed boys from the Black Forest, uncouth ones from the Allgäu region, with flaxen hair and wide mouths, energetic boys from the plains, open and light-hearted, refined types from Stuttgart with pointed shoes and an impure or rather over-refined dialect. Getting on for a fifth part of this flower of youth wore spectacles. One, a delicate, almost smartly dressed mother's boy from Stuttgart, was wearing a superior stiff felt hat; he bore himself proudly, blissfully unconscious of the fact that any peculiarity, even on the first day, would be noted and be the cause, later on, of ragging and bullying on the part of the bolder spirits.

A more discerning spectator would realize that this group of nervous boys was by no means an unrepresentative selection of the youth of the land. Alongside average boys, among whom the earnest plodder could easily be recognised, were a number of sensitive-looking or obstinately determined specimens whose smooth brows concealed dreams of a higher life. Perhaps there was one or more of those sly and stubborn Swabians among them like those who in the course of the years have, on occasion, been pressed into the service of the great world and made their inevitably somewhat dry and narrow ideas the focal point of some new and influential system of philosophy. For Swabia provides itself and the world not only with well-bred theologians but boasts a traditional aptitude for philosophical speculation which has on more than one occasion given birth to prophets of considerable importance, not to mention false prophets. And so this fruitful province whose politically great traditions stretch back into the past still exerts its influence on the world, at any rate in the spiritual domain of religious philosophy. Side by side with it there has long existed among the inhabitants a joy in beautiful form and dreamy poetry that likewise goes back into the past which has now and again produced poets and versifiers whose efforts are by no means without merit.

Superficially there was no trace of any Swabian element in the customs and organization of the Maulbronn Theological College; on the contrary a number of classical labels had recently been pasted up among the Latin names left over from monastic times. The Studies among which the pupils were divided bore the names Forum, Hellas, Athens, Sparta, Acropolis, and the fact that the smallest and last was called Germania might have been taken to indicate that they had reason for linking up present-time Germany as far as possible with a Graeco-Roman ideal. But even this was only superficially and in reality Hebraic names would have been more relevant. For as chance would have it, the study designated Athens, far from receiving the most broad-minded and eloquent members had a number of honest bores allotted to it and Sparta was not the home of warriors and ascetics but of a handful of respectable and fussy pupils housed there to attend outside lectures. Hans Giebenrath was put in Hellas together with a group of nine other companions.

A strange feeling came over him as with the other nine he entered the chilly and bare-looking dormitory in the evening for the first time and lay down in his narrow school bed. From the ceiling hung a large oil lamp whose red light served them to undress by and which was extinguished by the student teacher at a quarter past ten. The beds were ranged side by side and between each pair stood a small chair on which the boys piled their clothes; by the pillar hung the rope which rang the morning bell. Two or three of the boys had already become acquainted and exchanged a few timid whispers that very soon ceased altogether; the rest of them were strangers to each other and lay in their beds quiet and depressed. The ones already asleep breathed deeply and as they moved an arm in their sleep, the counterpane gave a faint rustling sound. Those who were still awake, kept quite still. Hans was unable to get off to sleep for a long time. He listened to the breathing of his neighbour and after a while caught an oddly frightened noise from the next bed but one; a boy was lying there, weeping with his sheet pulled over his head. This muffled sobbing affected Hans strangely. He himself was not suffering from home sickness and yet he was missing the quiet little room which he had at home; in addition there was a nervous apprehension of his novel situation and all the new faces. It was not yet midnight but no one else in the dormitory was awake. Young sleepers lay side by side, their cheeks pressed into the striped pillows, the sad and defiant, the faithful and timid, all overcome by the same sweet, untroubled repose and oblivion. A pale half-moon climbed above the steep old roofs, towers, bow windows, turrets, battlements and gothic arcades; its light lay across cornices, and window-ledges, poured over gothic windows and romanesque gateways and shimmered golden in the large, handsome bowl of the cloister fountain. A few yellow beams and flecks of light also fell into the Hellas dormitory through the three windows and formed as neighbourly an accompaniment to the dreams of the slumbering boys as it had to the monks in the old days.

The following day the solemn initiation ceremony took place in the Oratory. Teachers stood in their frock coats, the Principal gave the address; the students sat in the pews, bowed in thought and stole an occasional glance at their parents who were sitting a long way behind them. The mothers smiled wistfully at their sons, the fathers sat very erect and followed the discourse with grim seriousness. Proud and praiseworthy feelings and high hopes filled their breasts, and it did not occur to any one of them that he was exchanging his child for a financial advantage. At length one after the other each pupil was summoned by name and stood up before the rest, was given the ceremonial handshake by the Principal as a pledge on the part of the establishment that, provided he comported himself properly, he would be cared for and sheltered by the State for the remainder of his life. None of them seemed to realize—the fathers least of all—that they could not quite expect all that for nothing.

When the time came round for the boys to say goodbye to their mothers and fathers, it was a much sadder business. Some on foot, some by coach, some in any kind of transport they had been able to find in their haste were now disappearing from the view of their abandoned offspring and continued to wave their handkerchiefs for a long time in the mild September air until the forest finally swallowed up the travellers and their sons returned quiet and thoughtful to the monastery.

"Well, your parents have gone off now," remarked the student teacher. They began to size each other up and to try to become better acquainted, beginning with the boys in their own study. They filled the inkwells, lamps, put their texts and exercise books in order and tried to make themselves at home in their new common-room. They inspected each other eagerly in the process, started up conversations, asked each other what place and school they came from, reminded each other of the torture they had all been through in the *Landexamen*. Knots of chatting boys grouped themselves round isolated desks and now and again there rose the clear, ringing sound of boyish laughter, and by evening the members of each Study knew each other far better than travellers at the end of a long sea voyage.

Among the nine friends who shared Hellas with Hans were four real characters; the rest of them were undistinguished. First there was Otto Hartner, the son of a Stuttgart professor, gifted, calm, self-assured and exemplary in behaviour. He was already broad, handsome and well-dressed and impressed the Study with his firm, resolute step. Then there was Karl Hamel, the son of a small village mayor from the Swabian Uplands. It took a little time to get to know him for he was full of contradictions and rarely emerged from his apparent stolidity. When he did, he became impassioned, boisterous and violent but he very soon calmed down again and then it was hard to discover whether he was a quiet observer or merely a sly-boots.

Hermann Heilner was a striking though ingenuous person who came from a good family in the Black Forest. It was obvious from the first day that he was a poet and

67

scholar; the legend ran that he had written his composition in the *Landexamen* in hexameters. He was an energetic and eloquent talker, possessed a beautiful violin and gave one the impression that one could read his character which consisted chiefly of a youthfully immature mixture of sentimentality and light-heartedness like an open book. Yet there was a less superficial side to it which he kept hidden away. He was developed physically and mentally beyond his years and he was already beginning to move along experimental tracks of his own making.

The oddest boy in Hellas, however, was Emil Lucius, reserved, flaxen-haired, shy, hard-working and as dry as an old grey peasant. Despite his undeveloped stature and features he did not give the impression of being a boy; he had something grown up about him as if he was unlikely to change any more. Even on the first day while the others were bored or chattered and tried to settle in, he sat calm and collected over a grammar book, put his hands over his ears and studied as if he had whole lost years to make up.

The others gradually became familiar with the ways of this quiet boy and found him to be so expert in his meanness and egoism that his perfection in these vices compelled if not their respect at least a degree of tolerance. He had evolved a cunning saving and profit scheme, the detailed subtleties of which only came to light gradually and aroused much astonishment. It began first thing in the morning when they got up. Lucius would make a point of being either first or last in the wash-room in order that he might commandeer somebody else's towel and—if possible —soap and thereby keep his own towel in use for two or more weeks. The towels were supposed to be renewed every week and every Monday morning the student teacher checked them over. Lucius therefore used to hang a fresh towel on his numbered peg and fetch it away again during the lunch interval. He then folded it up, still unused and returned it to his box and hung the old one he had saved in its place. His soap was hard and it was difficult to get any off for a lather; so it lasted for months. Despite all this, Emil Lucius was by no means slovenly in appearance; on the contrary he always looked tidy, his soft blond hair was carefully combed and parted and he looked after his linen and clothes in exemplary fashion.

After they had washed, the next item was breakfast, which consisted of a cup of coffee, a lump of sugar and a roll. Most of the boys—having the hearty appetite of their age after eight hours' sleep—did not consider it at all wonderful. Lucius however found nothing to complain of; saved his daily lump of sugar and never failed to find someone to buy it from him at two bits a penny or twenty-five lumps for an exercise book. It was not surprising that he had a predilection for working by other boys' lamps in the evening in order to economise in expensive lamp-oil. Far from being the child of poor parents, he had been brought up in comfortable circumstances and knew how to live in a frugal and parsimonious way rarely achieved by the children of really poor people, living as they do from hand to mouth.

Not content with his scheming for material possessions and tangible goods Emil Lucius sought to exploit the advantages he had in the realm of the intellect where he was no less expert. While doing this, he was shrewd enough never to forget that intellectual possession is only of relative value; consequently he reserved his real efforts for the subjects likely to prove fruitful in the next examination, contenting himself with a modest average mark in the others. Whatever he learned or achieved he measured only by the performances of his schoolfellows and he would rather be first in a subject with an imperfect knowledge than second with twice the amount. With the result that you could see him sitting quietly at his work in the evening while his friends were devoting themselves to all kinds of pastimes, games and reading. He was not at all put out by the noise the others made, he merely gave an occasional, self-satisfied glance at them, for if they all worked at the same time as he did, his extra pains would have brought him no reward.

No one looked askance at all these sly dodges on the part of this industrious go-getter. But like all those who try to outdo and exploit their fellows, before long he made a fool of himself. As all instruction in the College was gratuitous, he thought he would turn this fact to advantage and take violin lessons. Not that he had any predisposition, ear or gift for music or even derived any pleasure from listening. But he was under the impression that you could learn to play the violin in the same way as you learn Latin or Mathematics. Music, he had heard, was useful in later life and brought favour on its exponents and in any case it did not cost anything since the College provided instruments for the pupils' use.

The music master's hair stood on end when Lucius came to him desiring to take music for Herr Hasse already knew him from the singing lessons when Lucius' performances greatly diverted his fellow pupils but drove him, the teacher, to despair. He did his utmost to dissuade the boy but with Lucius this was impossible for the boy merely gave a sly and modest smile, referred to his right to have lessons and expatiated on his intense passion for music. He was allotted one of the worst practice-violins and received two lessons a week and practised half-an-hour a day. After his first efforts, however, his Study companions declared that it was going to be the first and last time and they refused to let him continue to produce such unearthly noises. From then on Lucius would stroll restlessly down the cloisters searching out some corner where he might practice and from wherever that chanced to be, strange scraping, squeaking and whining sounds arose greatly to the disturbance of the neighbourhood. It was, remarked Heilner, the poet among them, as if the tortured instrument was desperately begging for mercy from all its old worm-holes. As Lucius was making no progress whatsoever, his pained teacher became more nervy and outspoken. Lucius practised with increasing desperation and his shopkeeper's face, hitherto so smooth and untroubled began to be lined with anxiety. It was tragic, for when his teacher finally proclaimed him utterly incapable and refused to continue with the lessons, the thwarted enthusiast elected to learn the piano and gave himself up to long, fruitless months of torture until he was worn out and quietly abandoned it. In later years, however, when music was being discussed, he would allow it to be known that he too had learned the piano and violin and it had only been untoward circumstances that had estranged him from those fine arts.

Hellas study frequently amused itself at the expense of its inhabitants for even the intellectual Heilner took part in many rags. Karl Hamel played the role of ironical and witty observer. He was a year older than the others, and gained a certain consideration from this fact though he made no attempt to exploit it or enhance his dignity in any way; he was moody and about once a week felt the urge to put his physical strength to the test in a " fight " when he would become violent almost to the point of cruelty.

Hans Giebenrath watched him in astonishment and went on his way, a good but peaceable comrade. He worked hard, almost as hard as Lucius, and enjoyed the respect of his fellow study companions with the exception of Heilner who had gained a reputation for ingenious levity and jeered at him for being a " swot." But on the whole most of them got along together well enough during this period of rapid development in their lives, even if nocturnal rags in the dormitories were a common occurrence. For they were eager to feel themselves grown-up and justify the respectful and still novel form of address used by the teacher through their systematic seriousness and good behaviour, and they looked back on the classical school they had just left with as much sympathetic derision as a university freshman on his grammar school days. But every now and then a natural boyishness burst through all this artificial dignity and clamoured for an outlet. Then the dormitory would resound once more with the trample of feet and boyish oaths.

It must be instructive and valuable for the principal or a teacher in an institution of this kind to consider how, after the first weeks of community life the horde of boys resembles a chemical mixture in which clouds and flakes in suspension come together, separate again, form other compounds until it results in a number of chemical compositions. After the boys had got over their first shyness and had all become sufficiently acquainted with each other, there was a general stir-round; groups came together, friendships and antipathies sprang up. It was unusual for fellow townsmen and former pupils from the same school to link up; they mostly cast about for new friends—town-dwellers turned to peasants' sons, boys from the Wurtemberg Uplands to boys from the plain, actuated by the unconscious attraction towards differences and complementaries. The boys groped their way hesitantly in these friendships; their recognition of likenesses was closely followed by their demands for differences, and in many of the boys germination of personality was now beginning for the first time. Strange little scenes of affection and jealousy took place, developed or open hostility and ended—as the case might be—in touching relationships and walks together or violent scraps and exchanges of blows.

Hans had no outward part in these affairs. Karl Hamel had offered his friendship with unequivocal impetuosity but Hans had shrunk back frightened. Immediately afterwards Hamel had become friendly with an inmate of Sparta and Hans was left on his own. He was strongly predisposed to see the land of friendship rise up on the sky-line in glowing colours; quietly but irresistibly it drew him on. But his shyness held him back. His gift for forging ties of affection had been thwarted in the grim days of his motherless childhood and he now felt a horror of all outward demonstrativeness. Further there was his boyish pride and painful urge to excel to be reckoned with. He was different from Lucius; he was really keen on knowledge for its own sake but like the latter he tried to avoid anything that might distract him from his work. Thus he would linger on industriously at his desk though not without a pang of envy and longing as he saw the others enjoying their friendship. Karl Hamel had been the wrong one but if anyone else had come along and had exerted any force of attraction he would have gladly followed. He sat waiting like a shy girl until someone should come and fetch him, some stronger, more courageous boy than himself who would take him along and compel him into happiness.

As there was much to do, especially in Hebrew, in their programme of work, these early days went by very quickly for the boys. The numerous small lakes and ponds with which Maulbronn is surrounded, reflected pale late-autumn skies, yellowing ash-trees, silver birches and oaks and a lengthening dusk; the last pre-winter rout had swept with exulting moans through the forests and there had already been several light hoar-frosts.

The romantic Hermann Heilner who had tried in vain to find a congenial companion now strode daily by himself through the woods in his free time and was particularly attracted by the forest-lake, a brown, melancholy stretch of water surrounded by reeds and overhung with the fading foliage of ancient trees. The sad beauty of this corner of the woods made an irresistible appeal to the sensitive boy. Here he could dreamily draw rings in the still water with a twig, recite Lenau's " Reed-songs " and as he lay among the rushes reflect on the autumnal theme of the dying year while a shower of leaves came down and the leafless tree-tops sighed in melancholy harmony. Then he would pull a notebook out of his pocket to scribble a few verses in it.

He was thus occupied one grey midday in late October when Hans Giebenrath, also walking on his own, happened on the same place. He saw the boy poet sitting on the plank of the small sluice-board with his notebook on his knee and his sharpened pencil stuck pensively in his mouth. A book lay open beside him. Slowly he approached him.

" Hello, Heilner. What are you doing ? "

" Reading Homer; and you, young Giebenrath ? "

" I don't believe you . . . I think I know what you're doing."

" Oh ? "

" Of course. You've been writing poetry."

" Do you think so ? "

" Of course."

" Sit here."

Giebenrath sat down next to Heilner on the plank, let his legs dangle over the water and watched one yellow leaf after another whirl down through the quiet, cool air, and silently land on the brown surface.

" It's sad here," said Hans.

" Yes."

They had both lain full length on their backs so that only a few overhanging tree-tops were visible and the pale-blue sky was revealed with its peaceful islands of clouds.

" What marvellous clouds," said Hans, gazing up luxuriously.

" Yes, young Giebenrath," said Heilner with a sigh, " if only we could be clouds like that."

" Then what ? "

" Why then we would sail along, over woods and villages, estates and provinces, like marvellous ships. Haven't you ever seen a ship ? "

" No, Heilner. And you ? "

" Yes, I have. But heavens above, what do you know about such things ! As long as you can swot and drudge away you're all right ! "

" You look on me as a fool, don't you ? "

" I've said so, haven't I ! "

" I haven't been as stupid as you think for some time now. But go on telling me about ships."

75

Heilner rolled over, nearly falling into the water in the process. He now lay prone on his belly, his chin cupped between his hands.

" I have seen boats on the Rhine," he went on, " during the holidays. One Sunday there was music on the ship and at night there were coloured lanterns. The lights were reflected in the water and we went downstream to the sound of music. We had Rhein wine to drink and the girls wore white dresses."

Hans listened and gave no reply, but he had closed his eyes and he could see the boats travelling through the summer night with music and lights and girls in white dresses. The other continued.

" Yes; how different from now. Who is there here who knows about such things ? They are all bores and sneaks ! They work and drudge away and the high-light of their knowledge is the Hebrew alphabet. And you are no different."

Hans was silent. This Heilner was a strange fellow. An enthusiast, a poet. He had often wondered about him before. Heilner did precious little work, it was well known, but nevertheless he knew a great deal and although he despised all this knowledge gave good answers.

" Here we read Homer," he continued with withering scorn, " as if the Odyssey was a cookery book, two lines per hour and then it is all chewed over and examined until we loathe the sight of it. And all the lessons end up the same way: " You see how well the poet has turned it. Here you have a glimpse into the secret of poetic creation ! " So much sugar round the particle and aorist pill so we can swallow it down without choking. You can take away the whole of Homer from me, at this price. What's this old Greek stuff to do with us, anyway ? If any of us wanted to try and live according to the Greek way of life, he would be flung out. And that's why our Study is called Hellas ! ! What an insult. Why not call it ' Waste-paper basket ' ' Slave-cage ' or ' Torture Chamber ? ' The whole classics business is a swindle." He spat into the air.

" You've written poetry before, haven't you ? " asked Hans.

" Yes."

" What about ? "

" This spot; about the lake and autumn."

" Show me it."

" No; it's not yet finished."

" But when it is."

" Yes; if you like."

They both got up and strolled back to the monastery.

" Have you ever really noticed how beautiful it all is ? " asked Heilner, as they went past the ' Galilee '— halls, bow windows, cloisters, refectories, gothic and romanesque, all so rich in craftsmanship. "And what is all this magic for ? For three dozen poor boobs who are intended for the church. The State needs them."

Hans thought about Heilner the whole afternoon. What sort of a chap was he ? He certainly did not share Hans' hopes and anxieties. He had thoughts and words of his own and he lived more intensely and more freely, suffered from strange troubles of his own and appeared to despise everything round about him. He understood the beauty of the old pillars and walls. And he practised the secretive and unusual art of expressing his emotions in verse and creating a world of his own from his imagination. He was restless and unruly and made more witticisms in one day than Hans did in a year. He was morose and appeared to luxuriate in his melancholy as if it was some strange and precious possession.

That same evening Heilner treated the whole Study to an example of his striking two-sided personality. One of his companions, a petty boaster named Otto Wagner, picked a quarrel with him. For a while Heilner kept calm, light-hearted and detached, then he allowed his temper to get the better of him and he struck his opponent on the ear. Immediately both boys lost their tempers and went for each other and soon became inextricably entangled; they lunged this way and that like a rudderless ship, now moving in half circles, now lurching through the Study by the walls, over chairs, along the floor, both fuming with rage and gasping for breath. Their friends looked on with critical eyes, giving the intertwined forms a wide berth, keeping their legs out of the way, saving their desks and lamps and awaiting the issue in cheerful excitement. A few minutes later Heilner rose painfully to his feet and stood there breathing hard. He looked strained, his eyes were bloodshot, his shirt collar was torn, and there was a tear in the knee of his trousers. His opponent was preparing to renew his attack but Heilner stood with folded arms and said scornfully, " I am willing to stop if you will; shake hands." Otto Wagner went off muttering. Heilner leant back in his desk, turned up his lamp, thrust his hands into his trouser pockets and had the air of wanting to think something out. Suddenly tears welled in his eyes and chased each other down his cheeks, faster and faster. It was a scandalous exhibition; weeping was considered the most unspeakable thing a student could do. Nor was he making any attempt to hide it. He did not leave the room, he stood still with his pale face turned towards the lamp; he did not wipe his tears or even take his hands out of his

78

pockets. The other boys stood round, staring at him, inquisitive and malicious until Hartner planted himself in front of him and said, " Eh, you, Heilner, aren't you ashamed of yourself ? "

The weeping boy glanced slowly round him, like some one waking out of a deep sleep.

" Ashamed—what in front of you ? " he said in loud, withering tones. " No, my good man."

He wiped his face, gave a bitter smile, blew out his lamp and left the room.

Hans Giebenrath had stayed in his place throughout the incident, content to steal frightened glances in Heilner's direction. A quarter of an hour later he ventured to follow him. He saw him sitting motionless in the dark and chilly dormitory looking down into the cloisters. His shoulders and his sharp narrow head had a peculiarly serious and unboylike air about them. He did not stir when Hans went up to him and stood by the window, and only after some time did he ask, without turning his head, in a husky voice.

" What's up ? "

" It's me," said Hans shyly.

" What do you want ? "

" Nothing."

" Oh, then you can go away again."

Hans was hurt and made to walk off but then Heilner held him back. " Stop, though," he said in a tone he endeavoured to made light-hearted, " I didn't mean it."

They looked at each other. It was probably the first time they had ever studied each other's face and felt that behind each other's smooth features lived an individual person, a kindred spirit, with his own peculiarities.

Slowly Hermann Heilner stretched out his arm, gripped Hans by the shoulder and drew him towards himself until their cheeks were quite close. Then Hans in a sudden exquisite panic felt his friend's lips touch his own.

His heart raced and there was an unaccustomed tightness in his chest. This being together in the dark dormitory and this sudden kiss was a novel, perhaps dangerous adventure; it occurred to him how dreadful it would have been to be caught in such an act, realizing intuitively that this kiss would appear much more of a joke and scandal than the weeping incident previously. He was unable to say a word but the blood rose to his cheeks and he felt an impulse to run away.

A grown-up, witnessing this little scene would possibly have taken a secret pleasure in this shy, awkward affection, this bashful declaration of friendship and in the two small boyish faces, pretty and full of promise with their childish sweetness flushed with the handsome defiance of adolescence.

Gradually all these young people were discovering each other in their common life together. They had got to know each other and had formed some idea of what their comrades were like, and a host of friendships were struck up. There were pairs of friends who learned Hebrew verbs together, pairs who sketched together, went for walks or read Schiller. There were good Latin scholars and bad mathematicians who had made friends with bad Latinists and good mathematicians in order to share the benefits of work done in common. There were friendships too based on a different kind of covenant, that of mutual ownership. Thus, the much-envied owner of the ham had found his complementary half in a gardener's son from Stammheim whose tuck-box was full of choice apples. On one occasion when he got thirsty eating ham he asked the other for an apple and offered him some ham in exchange. They sat together and embarked on a cautious conversation of which the general gist was that the ham would be replaced as soon as it was finished and that the apple owner would be able to go on drawing on his father's supplies well into the New Year. Thus a solid understanding resulted between them which long outlasted many more idealistic and impetuous pacts of friendship.

There were very few who had not paired off but Lucius, whose acquisitive devotion to art was then at its height, was one of them.

There were also some ill-matched pairs, the striking example of which was provided by Hermann Heilner and Hans Giebenrath — the frivolous and the conscientious, poet and striver. Both were considered clever and exceptionally gifted but whereas Heilner rejoiced in the half derisive appellation of genius, to Hans was attached the odium of being a model boy. Yet they were left comparatively unmolested, each being taken up with their own friendship and each liking to keep to himself.

However, despite all these personal complications and events the College did not come off too badly since it set the pace and rhythm compared with which Lucius' music, Heilner's verses, all the vows of friendship, material transactions and occasional exchange of blows were merely insignificant diversions. And in particular there was always this question of Hebrew. That strange and ancient language of Jehovah, harsh yet mysteriously alive, loomed up difficult and baffling before the eyes of these students, striking in its amazing ramifications, delighting by its remarkably coloured and fragrant blossoms. Thousand-year old spirits peopled its branches, some fear-inspiring, some friendly, fantastically terrifying dragons, naive and attractive legends, wrinkled, grave desiccated grey-beards alongside handsome boys and quiet-eyed girls or war-like women. Words that had sounded distant and dreamy in the Lutheran Bible now became a thing of flesh and blood in the powerful original and took on a ponderously archaic but tough and sinister reality. That, at any rate, was how it appeared to Heilner who daily and hourly cursed the whole Pentateuch and yet found more life and soul in it and got more out of it than many painstaking learners who had mastered their vocabulary and had got beyond the stage of making mistakes in reading.

Alongside this, the New Testament where things moved more tenderly and lightly and whose language was indeed, if not so ancient, deep and rich, filled him with a young, eager and even dreamy spirit of unreality.

And the Odyssey from whose strong, ringing symmetrical verses rose, like the white, rounded arm of a water nymph, knowledge and feeling about a vanished life with its clear contours and its happiness, sometimes firm and comprehensible in boldly drawn outlines, at others glowing like a secret and half-guessed dream from a few words and lines.

The historians Xenophon and Livy were also there as minor luminaries, modest and almost insignificant in comparison.

Hans was surprised to notice how different it all seemed to his friends. For Heilner nothing was abstract; nothing existed that he personally could not evoke or paint with the colours of his imagination. Subjects where his methods did not work he abandoned with distaste. Mathematics for him was a sphinx charged with treacherous riddles whose cold and evil glance fascinated her victims, and he gave this monster a wide berth.

The relationship between the two friends was an odd

one. For Heilner the friendship was a pleasure, a luxury, a comfort or a mood, but for Hans at one moment it was a proudly guarded treasure, at another, an overwhelming burden. So far Hans had always made use of the evening for his work. Now, however, practically every day Hermann came over to see him when he had had enough of the day's drudgery; he snatched his book away from him and completely monopolized him. Finally Hans began to tremble every evening just before Hermann was due to arrive, so dear had his friend become, and toiled with redoubled zeal and speed in the compulsory preparation period so as not to lose ground with his work. It was still more distressing to him when Heilner began to attack his zest for work with argument as well. " It's just hackwork; you do all your work freely and voluntarily but fundamentally it's out of fear of your teachers or your old man. What do you get out of it whether you come first or second ? I am twentieth but I'm no more stupid than you mark-grubbers."

Hans was also horrified when he first noticed how Heilner treated his text-books. On one occasion he had left his own books behind in the lecture-room and wishing to prepare the next geography lesson, had borrowed Heilner's atlas. He was disgusted to see that the latter had covered whole pages with pencilled scribble. The west coast of the Spanish peninsula had been distorted into a grotesque profile in which the nose reached from Oporto to Lisbon and the Cape Finisterre region had been stylised into a curly wig, while Cape St. Vincent formed the beautifully twisted point of a man's beard. It went on like this for page after page; caricatures were drawn on the backs of the maps and insulting and comic rhymes were written and they were covered with blots. Hans was accustomed to treat his books as sacred possessions and this disrespect seemed to him partly a desecration of the holy of holies, partly a criminal yet heroic act.

One might form the impression that the exemplary Giebenrath was really only an agreeable toy for his friend, a kind of house cat, and Hans himself sometimes felt this to be the case. But Heilner clung to him because he needed him. He had to have someone, a confidant, an audience, someone to admire him. He needed someone to listen calmly and eagerly when he made fiery attacks on the College and life in general. He also needed someone who could comfort him, someone in whose lap he could lay his head in his moments of depression. Like all such natures, the young poet suffered from attacks of a mysterious, somewhat vain melancholy the causes of which lie partly in the gentle leave-taking from childish things, partly in the as yet purposeless exuberance of animal spirits, vague longings and desires, partly the mysterious growth into manhood. And he also had an unhealthy craving for sympathy and affection. Earlier in his life he had been a mother's darling and now, still unripe for a girl's love, his accommodating friend played the role of comforter.

He often came to Hans in the evening, greatly depressed, snatched his work away from him and got him to accompany him to the dormitory. There in the cold room or in the lofty oratory they walked to and fro in the twilight or sat shivering in a window embrasure. On these occasions Heilner would give tongue to all sorts of grievances in the manner of romantic youths enamoured of Heine, and seemed enveloped in clouds of a childish sadness which Hans could not quite fathom, though it impressed and sometimes infected him. The sensitive intellectual, Heilner, was particularly liable to these moods in grey weather and his moans and complaints would reach their climax in the evenings when late autumn rain clouds obscured the sky and the moon pursued its course behind them, peering through the veil and cloud-rifts. Then he would indulge in this Ossianesque mood which found expression in sighs, speeches and poems which he poured out to the innocent Hans.

Pained and oppressed by these sorrowful scenes, Hans plunged for the remaining hours into work which he was finding increasingly difficult. He was no longer surprised to have a recurrence of his headaches; but he was greatly distressed to find himself spending weary and ineffectual hours in this way and then having to drive himself on to make up the necessary work. Indeed he had an obscure feeling that his friendship with his erratic friend was exhausting him and playing havoc with a part of his being which previously had been undisturbed; but the more morose and tearful his friend was, the more upset he felt and at the same time the more touched and proud at being thus indispensable to his friend.

At the same time he realized that this sickly melancholy was only the expression of an exaggerated and unhealthy instinct and did not really belong to Heilner's character which he loyally and genuinely admired. When his friend read out his poems, discussed his poetic ideals or spoke soliloquies from Schiller and Shakespeare with passion and grandiloquent gesture, Hans felt as if his friend by virtue of some magic gift which he himself lacked floated in the air, moved in a godlike freedom and fiery passion and soared above him and his kind on winged sandals like a Homeric messenger. Up to the present the poets' world had been little known to him and had seemed unimportant, but now he became aware of the treacherous power of fine sounding words, alluring imagery and soothing rhymes, and his respect for this newly-opened world had grown, with his admiration of his friend, into a single shared feeling.

Meantime, dark, turbulent November days arrived when it was only possible to work without lamps for a few hours a day, and black nights when the storm sent great rolling mountains of cloud over the veiled hills and beat, moaning and wailing round the ancient and stoutly built monastery walls. By this time the trees had completely shed their leaves; only the huge gnarled oaks, kings of that well-wooded landscape, rustled their dried tops in a louder and more surly tone than the rest of the trees. Heilner was utterly downcast and had recently taken to scraping away on his fiddle alone in a remote practice-room or engaging in squabbles with his companions instead of sitting with Hans.

One evening when he had gone to the music room he found the zealous Lucius busy practising in front of a music-stand. He turned away angrily and returned half an hour later. The latter was still at it.

"You might stop now," cursed Heilner. "There are other people who want to practise too. Your scraping is a menace."

Lucius refused to give way; Heilner turned nasty and when the other calmly resumed his scraping, he landed a kick at his music desk so that the sheets of music were scattered on the floor and the desk struck the player in the face. Lucius stooped down to retrieve the music.

"I shall report this to the Principal," he said firmly.

" Splendid," shrieked Heilner in a rage, " and you can also tell him that I kicked you as well, free of charge." He made as if to translate his words into action.

Lucius jumped aside and gained the door. His pursuer went after him and there followed a heated and noisy charge through the corridors and rooms, down staircases and across landings as far as the furthest wing of the establishment where the Principal's house stood in solitary splendour. Heilner caught the fugitive only just before the Principal's study door, and when the latter had already knocked and stood in the open entrance he received the promised kick at the last moment and burst like a bomb into the Principal's sanctum too panic-stricken to close the door behind him.

It was a scandalous incident. Next morning the Principal delivered a full-dress lecture on the degeneracy of youth; Lucius listened with thoughtful approval and Heilner heard his sentence, a long period of detention, read out. " Such a severe punishment has not been meted out here for years," thundered the Principal. " I am making sure that you will still remember it in ten years time. I am holding Heilner up to the rest of you as a terrible example."

The whole college stole a horrified glance at him as he stood there pale and defiant and met, unflinching, the Principal's gaze. A large number of the boys admired him secretly; nevertheless he was left alone and avoided like a leper at the end of the lesson when they all trooped noisily into the corridors. It needed courage to stand by him now.

Even Hans Giebenrath did not do so. He felt that he should have done, and his cowardice distressed him. Miserable and ashamed he squeezed into a window embrasure, unable to raise his eyes. He felt an impulse to seek out his friend, and he would have

given a great deal to have been able to do so unnoticed. But a boy who has received such a heavy
detention punishment is branded. Everybody else knows
that from now on the recipient will be under close observa-
tion and that it will be dangerous and gain one a bad
reputation to have any dealings with him. A severe and
ruthless discipline must be the price of the benefits
provided for the pupils by the State. The idea had already
been adumbrated in the famous inaugural address. Hans
was aware of this and he succumbed in this struggle
between loyalty to his friend and his wish to win a good
name. His ambition at present was to forge ahead, obtain
brilliant examination results and play some sort of role, not
a romantic or dangerous one, in the establishment. So he
lingered on in his corner. He could still come forward and
be brave but it was becoming more difficult every moment
and before he realized it, his treachery had become a
reality.

Heilner did not fail to notice it. The emotional boy
knew he was being shunned and understood, but he had
counted on Hans. His previous groundless feelings of
injury now seemed futile and grotesque compared with
his present distress and revulsion. He stood near Giebenrath for a moment, looking pale and proud and said in a
low voice, " You are a common coward, Giebenrath, the
devil you are ! " and he strode off, whistling between his
teeth and his hands thrust in his trousers' pocket.

It was a good thing that there were other thoughts and
occupations to claim the boys' attention. A few days after
this event there was a sudden fall of snow, followed by
clear frosty winter weather; they could snowball and skate
and they all suddenly realized that Christmas and the
holidays were upon them and did not cease talking about

it. They paid less attention to Heilner. He went around quiet and defiant with his head held high and a proud expression on his face; he spoke to no one and wrote verse in an exercise book that had a cover of black oil-cloth and bore the title " Songs of a Monk." Hoar frost and frozen snow hung in delicate, fantastic shapes on the oak trees, alders and willows. The clear ice crackled on the frozen ponds. The cloister garth looked like a silent garden of marble. A cheerful, festive excitement ran through all the Studies and anticipation of Christmas produced a glow of tolerance and gaiety even in the two staid and imperturbable professors. No one, whether teacher or pupil, was indifferent to Christmas and even Heilner began to look less pained and sullen and Lucius considered which books and pairs of shoes he would take away with him for the holidays. Agreeably ominous items began to appear in letters from home: questions about favourite wishes, reports of baking days, hints of coming surprises and joyful reunions.

The College and Hellas in particular experienced a slight diversion before their journeys home. It had been decided to invite the staff to an evening Christmas celebration which was to take place in Hellas, the largest of the Studies. A speech of welcome, two recitations, a flute solo and a violin duet were prepared. A humorous item was needed to complete the programme. The boys deliberated together, made and rejected proposals without reaching any agreement. Then Karl Hamel suggested that the best item to cheer things up would be a violin solo from Emil Lucius. The idea won acceptance. By dint of requests, promises and threats the wretched musician was driven to consent. And now on the programme which was sent out to the staff together with a polite invitation figured as a special number: "'Stille Nacht,' air for violin, Emil Lucius, Chamber music virtuoso." He owed this designation to his assiduous practising in the remote music room.

The Principal, masters, supervisors, music teacher, and student teacher were invited and duly appeared at the concert. The violin teacher's brow was bathed in sweat when Lucius made his entry, groomed and immaculate in a black tail-coat borrowed from Hartner, and wearing a modest smile on his face. Even the bow he now made was an invitation to levity. The air, " Stille Nacht " turned into a doleful dirge beneath his fingers; he made a false start, tortured and murdered the tune, beat the time out with his foot and attacked it with all the gusto of a man chopping trees down in frosty weather.

The Principal made a signal to the music master who had become pale with indignation.

When Lucius had begun for the third time and had got stuck again, he lowered his fiddle, turned towards the audience and apologized: " It's no use. But I have only been learning the violin since last autumn."

" That's fine, Lucius," called out the Principal, " we are obliged to you for your efforts. Stick to it. Per aspera ad astra."

On December 24th, from three o'clock in the morning onwards there was a great deal of noise and activity in all the dormitories. The hoar frost bloomed on the window panes in dense layers of patterned tracery, the water for washing in was frozen and a keen icy wind to which the boys remained oblivious, cut across the cloister. The large pans of coffee were steaming in the dining-hall and shortly afterwards dark bunches of schoolboys muffled up in coats and scarves were making their way to the distant railway station across the white, faintly glowing fields and through the silent woods. They were all chatting, making jokes and laughing loudly, yet each was inwardly taken up with his own private desires, pleasures and hopes. They knew that parents, brothers and sisters were waiting for them in warm, festive rooms, far away in the country, in towns, villages, and lonely farmsteads. For the majority it was the first Christmas for which they had travelled home from a distance, and most of them knew that their arrival was awaited with love and pride.

They waited for the train in the little station in the middle of the snow-covered wood and never before had they been so tolerant and cheerful and so much of one mind. Heilner was the only one who kept silent to himself when the train came in, waited until all his comrades had mounted and then climbed into another compartment on his own. Hans noticed him again when they changed at the next station but the feeling of shame and regret vanished in all the joy and excitement of the journey home.

He found his father in the house, smiling smugly, and a table generously covered with presents awaiting him. There was no real Christmas in the Giebenrath house. No carol singing or other festivities; no mother, no Christmas-tree. Herr Giebenrath did not understand the art of celebrating holidays. But he was proud of his son and he had not been mean with his presents on this occasion. And as Hans was not used to anything different, he had nothing to miss.

They thought he looked an unhealthy colour and was too thin and pale and supposed that the food provided was inadequate. But this he stoutly denied and assured them that he was quite well except for his frequent headaches. But the vicar consoled him on this point; he, too, had suffered from headaches in his younger days. So that was all in order.

The river was frozen hard and smooth and covered with people skating during the holiday period. Hans was on it almost all day long, wearing a new suit and his green theological college hat on his head; he had left his former schoolfellows behind and felt transported into an enviable and higher world.

CHAPTER FOUR

It usually happened that the College lost one or more members during their four-year period there. Sometimes a boy died and was buried to the singing of hymns or his body was taken home accompanied by a cortège of friends. Sometimes a boy would run away or be expelled for some outrageous offence. On rare occasions, and even then the experience was confined to the top forms, a desperate boy would find a quick solution to his adolescent problems by shooting himself or by jumping in the river.

The College was destined to lose some boys of Hans Giebenrath's year and by a strange coincidence they all belonged to Hellas.

Among the members of the latter was an unassuming, fair-haired boy, Hindinger, nicknamed " Hindu," the son of a tailor somewhere in the Protestant part of the Swabian Allgäu. Hindu was a peaceable citizen and his disappearance from their midst was the sole reason that he became—if only to a limited extent—a topic of conversation. As he shared a desk with the thrifty " chamber music " virtuoso, Lucius, he had, in his shy amiable way, slightly more to do with him than the rest of them had, but apart from Lucius, he had no other friends. Only when they had lost him did the members of Hellas notice that they had appreciated him as a good and unexacting neighbour and a soothing influence in the often noisy life of the Study.

One January day he had joined a party of skaters who had gone out to the horse-pond. He did not possess any skates himself but he was eager to go and watch the others.

However, he soon got chilly and stamped round on the bank to warm himself up. While so doing he gradually broke into a run and for a time lost his way across the fields and came upon another small lake which because of the warmer and stronger springs that supplied it, was only lightly frozen over. Hindinger walked out over the frozen reeds. Small and light though he was he disappeared through the ice near the bank, struggled and called for help for a short time and then sank back into the black coldness with no one there to see him.

It was not until two o'clock when the first afternoon lesson began that his absence was noticed.

" Where's Hindinger ? " shouted the young master.

Nobody answered.

" Have a look round Hellas ! "

But there was no trace of him there.

" He must have got delayed, let's start without him. Look, we are on page 74, line seven. I hope nothing like this will occur again. You must be punctual."

When it struck three o'clock and Hindinger was still missing, the master became nervous and sent to the Principal. That august person himself came to the classroom, started an intensive inquiry and sent out a search party of ten boys under the student teacher and a junior master. The rest of the class was set a written exercise to do.

At four o'clock the master re-entered the classroom without knocking and whispered something to the Principal.

" Silence ! " ordered the Principal, and the boys sat motionless in their seats and looked at him expectantly.

" Your friend Hindinger," he continued in a quieter tone, " appears to have got drowned in a pond. You must come and help to find him. Herr Professor Meyer will lead the party; you must obey his instructions and do nothing on your own initiative."

Frightened and whispering among themselves they started out with the master in front. A handful of men from the town, carrying ropes, laths and poles joined the hurrying procession. It was bitterly cold and the sun had already sunk to the rim of the forest.

By the time the small, stiff body of the boy was finally discovered and laid on a hurdle in the snow-covered rushes, it was already deep twilight. The boys stood round, frightened, like shy birds, staring at the corpse and rubbing their stiff blue fingers. Only when their drowned comrade was borne before them and they followed silently over the snowfields did a sudden shudder run through their chilled hearts and they scented death as a deer scents its enemy.

Hans Giebenrath chanced to be next to his former friend, Heilner, in the sorrowful and frozen band. Both became aware of their proximity at the same moment as they were stumbling over the rough ground in the open field. It might be that the sight of death had overpowered him and convinced him momentarily of the futility of all ambition; whatever the reason when Hans unexpectedly found his friend's pale face so close to him, he felt an inexplicable, deep sorrow and in a fit of emotion he tentatively grasped Heilner's hand. But Heilner withdrew his angrily and darted an offended, sidelong look at Hans, then sought out another place in the procession and disappeared to the rear.

The heart of the exemplary Hans beat in sorrow and shame and he could not check his tears which poured down his cheeks blue with frost as he stumbled on over the frozen fields. He now realised that there are sins and

95

omissions that you can never forget and that no repentance can set right, and he had the feeling that it was not the little tailor's son who lay on the bier they bore on their shoulders but his friend Heilner and that he was taking his sorrow and anger at his treachery with him into another world where people are not judged by certificates and examinations and successes but according to the pure or blemished state of their conscience.

Meantime the procession had reached the main road and before long they were back in the College where all the teachers, headed by the Principal, were there to receive the dead Hindinger who in his lifetime would have run a mile to avoid such an honour. Schoolmasters look at a dead schoolboy very differently from the way they regard a living one; they are convinced, for the moment, of the worth and uniqueness of every individual life in their charge and every youthtime against which they sin with such indifference the rest of the time.

But that evening and the whole of the next day the presence of the frail corpse worked like a magic spell, damped down and subdued all activity and conversation so that for a brief interlude all wrangling, anger, noise and laughter were hidden away like water sprites who disappear momentarily from the surface of the water and leave it calm and apparently uninhabited. Whenever two people spoke together of the drowned boy they called him by his full name, for the nickname Hindu did not seem dignified enough now the boy was dead. And the quiet Hindu who had been wont to merge unnoticed into the crowd now filled the whole establishment with his name and his dead presence.

Herr Hindinger arrived on the second day, stayed a few hours alone in the little room where his son lay, was then invited to tea by the Principal and spent the night at the Stag.

Then came the funeral. The coffin was placed in the dormitory and the tailor from the Swabian Allgäu stood beside it, staring at them all. He was a typical tailor, terribly thin and bony and he wore a black frock coat, now green with age, and narrow, meanly cut trousers; in his hand he held an old-fashioned top hat which he reserved for festive occasions. His narrow, thin face looked sad, distressed and fragile like a ship's riding-light in a tempest and he stood there in a permanent state of embarrassment and awe before the Principal and the rest of the staff.

At the last minute before the bearers took up the coffin, this wistful little man came forward once again and touched the lid of the coffin with a puzzled and shy gesture of tenderness. He stood there helpless, fighting against his tears in the middle of the vast, quiet room like a withered tree in winter so abandoned and wretched that one could hardly bear to look at this victim of circumstance. The vicar took him by the hand and stood beside him, then he donned his fantastic stiff hat and led the funeral procession down the stairs, across the cloister garth through the ancient gateway and over the whitened earth in the direction of the low graveyard wall. During the singing of the hymn by the graveside most of the boys, to the annoyance of the music master who was conducting, did not watch his hand as he beat time; they gazed instead at the unsteady form of the little tailor who stood, chilly and dejected, listening with bowed head to the orations of the vicar, the Principal and the top boy, nodded absently at the singing schoolboys and fumbled now and again in his coat pocket with his left hand for the handkerchief he had

97

tucked away but without ever succeeding in pulling it out.

" I could not help imagining how it would be if it had been my own father standing there," said Otto Hartner afterwards. The other boys agreed, " Yes; that's what I thought too."

Later on the Principal brought Hindinger's father into Hellas. " Is there anyone here who was a particular friend of the dead boy ? " the Principal asked the Study. At first nobody replied, and Hindu's father looked into the young faces, pained and nervous. Then Lucius stepped forward and Hindinger took his hand and grasped it firmly for a short time. But he did not know what to say and left the room shortly afterwards nodding his head humbly. Then he started off for the long day's journey he must make through the clear winter landscape before he reached home and could describe to his wife the little spot where their Karl now lay buried.

The spell was broken in the College. The teachers were already grumbling at the boys again and little thought was spared for the boy who had now left Hellas for ever. Some of their number had caught chills through having stood about so long by the gloomy pond and were now in the sickroom or running about in felt slippers, their necks enveloped in scarves. Hans Giebenrath, however, had nothing wrong with his feet or neck but the expression on his face was older and more serious since the day of the fatality. A change had come over him; a boy had turned into a youth, and his spirit had likewise been transferred to another world where it fluttered timidly and ill at ease unable to find anywhere to rest. It was not the consequence either of fear of death or grief over the worthy Hindu but of his feeling of guilt towards Heilner which had suddenly sprung to life.

The latter was in the sickroom with two other boys; he had to swallow down hot tea and there was an opportunity for him to sort out his impressions over the death of Hindinger possibly for future poetic use. But he showed little inclination to do so. He looked much more wretched and ill than ever and hardly exchanged a word with his fellow invalids. His period of enforced isolation since his punishment detention had wounded and embittered a sensitive temperament that was in such great need of sympathetic understanding. The teachers regarded him sternly as a discontent and rebel; the other boys avoided him, the student teacher treated him with derisive amiability but those kindred spirits, Shakespeare and Schiller and Lenau had revealed a greater and nobler world than the oppressive and discouraging one that hedged him in at present. His "Monk's Songs" which had at first been written in the melancholy mood of a recluse gradually turned into a collection of cynical and virulent satires on the College, teachers and pupils. He found a bitter, martyrlike satisfaction in his isolation, enjoyed being misunderstood and thought of himself as a minor Juvenal in his mercilessly derisive Monk's verses.

A week after the funeral when both friends had recovered and Heilner was the only one still in bed in the sickroom, Hans paid him a visit. He greeted him shyly, pulled a chair up to the bed, sat down, stretched his hand out to the sick boy who turned angrily to the wall and seemed completely unapproachable. But Hans refused to be put off. He gripped his hand tightly and forced his former friend to look at him. The latter pulled a wry face.

"What do you want then?"

Hans did not release his hand.

"You must listen to me," he said. "I have been a coward to let you down. But you know how it is with me; it was my firm resolve to be among the first few places in the College and if possible to be first. You called it mark-grubbing; rightly as far as I'm concerned, but it was at that time the the kind of ideal I had set before me; I did not know of anything better."

Heilner had closed his eyes and Hans proceeded quietly, "You see, I feel upset. I do not know whether you will ever be my friend again but at least I must have your forgiveness."

Heilner was silent and did not open his eyes. The good and happy elements in his character rejoiced within him but he had grown accustomed to assuming the role of the callous and solitary soul; at any rate this was the mask he wore on some occasions, but Hans was not to be put off.

"You've got to, Heilner! I would rather drop to the bottom of the class than have to keep running round you like this. If you will agree, we will be friends again and show the others that we don't need them."

Then Heilner returned the pressure of his hand and opened his eyes.

A few days after this he got up and left the sickroom. This newly-struck friendship caused considerable excitement in the College. The weeks that now ensued were wonderful for both of them; though nothing happened in particular, both boys were filled with a strangely happy feeling of harmony and silent and secret understanding. It was quite different from before. Their long estrangement had changed them both. Hans had become warmer, more affectionate and enthusiastic; Heilner had developed a stronger, more manly personality and both had missed each other so much in recent weeks that their reunion assumed the importance of a great event, a priceless gift.

Full of shy misgiving, the two precocious boys were enjoying an unconscious foretaste of the tender secrets of a first love. The bond between them had all the harsh excitement of adolescence with the added attraction that lay in their mutual defiance of the rank and file of their schoolfellows. The latter, whose own innumerable friendships had not passed the stage of casual amusement considered Heilner disagreeable and Hans incomprehensible.

The more closely and contentedly Hans clung to his friendship the more alien the school seemed. The novel feeling of happiness coursed through his blood and brain like new wine and Livy no less than Homer lost his importance and thrill. The masters were horror-stricken to see the once exemplary Giebenrath transformed into a problem child and falling under the bad influence of the highly suspect Heilner. There is in fact nothing that horrifies the schoolmaster so much as those strange creatures, precocious boys in the already dangerous period of adolescence. Further, a certain element of genius had already seemed unwholesome to them in Heilner, for there exists a traditional hiatus between genius and the teaching profession and any hint of that element in schoolboys is regarded by them with horror from the very first. As far as they are concerned geniuses are those misguided pupils who never show them any proper respect, begin to smoke at the age of fourteen, fall in love at fifteen, go to pubs at sixteen, read forbidden books, write scandalous essays, stare at their teacher with withering scorn and are noted down in the school day-book as trouble-makers and candidates for detention. A schoolmaster would rather have a whole class of duffers than one genius, and strictly speaking he is right, for his task is not to educate unusual boys but to produce good Latinists, mathematicians, and good honest fools. Which of the two suffers most, the master at the hands of the boy or conversely, which is the greater tyrant or tormenter and which of the two it is who destroys and profanes, partially at any rate, the life and spirit of the other, it is impossible to judge without thinking back to one's own youth with anger and shame. But that is not our present concern, and we have the comfort of knowing that in true geniuses the wounds almost always heal, and they become people who create their master-pieces in spite of school and who later, when they are dead and the pleasant aura of remoteness hangs over them, are held up by schoolmasters to succeeding generations as exemplary and noble beings. And so the spectacle of the perpetual battle between regulation and spirit is repeated in each school in turn, and we continue to watch the State and school eagerly occupied in nipping in the bud the handful of profounder and nobler spirits who grow up year by year. And it is still especially the boys who are always in trouble, the ones who run away or are expelled who seem destined to enrich the life of their country when they are older. Nevertheless many—and who can tell their number—waste away in mute rebellion and finally go under.

In accordance with the good traditional school principle, not sympathy but sternness was increased towards our two young eccentrics once they fell under suspicion. Only the Principal, who was proud of Hans as a hard-working Hebraist, made a clumsy effort at rescuing him. He summoned him to his study, the lovely, picturesque, bow-windowed room of the old prior's house in which, so the legend ran, Faustus who lived in the neighbouring town of Knittlingen, had enjoyed many a beaker of Elfinger wine. The Principal was a reasonable person; he did not lack insight and practical wisdom; he was even favourably disposed towards his pupils whom he liked to address on terms of friendly condescension. His chief fault was an overweening vanity which frequently led him to indulge in excessive displays of cleverness from his dais and would not allow him to brook any interference with or questioning of his authority. He could not take a reproach or admit a mistake. Thus the weaker or less honest boys came off well but the stronger and more forthright personalities fared badly since he became excited at the slightest hint of a contradiction. He was adept at playing the role of paternal friend with the encouraging expression and the proper tone of affection, and this was the role he now assumed.

" Be seated, Giebenrath," he said amiably, after giving the boy who had just shyly entered a hearty handshake. " I would like to have a friendly chat with you, if I may."

" Please, Sir."

" You yourself will have felt, no doubt, my dear Gieben- rath, that your work has suffered somewhat recently—in Hebrew, at any rate. You used to be perhaps our best Hebrew scholar. I am sorry therefore to notice a sudden falling-off. Possibly you are not enjoying the subject any more ? "

" Oh, but I am, Sir."

" Think about it. These things do happen, you know. Perhaps you are giving some other subject your particular attention at the moment ? "

" No, Sir."

" Are you sure ? Well, we must look for other causes then. Can you help to put me on the track ? "

" I don't know . . . I have always done the work set . . ."

" Indeed you have, my dear boy. But differendum est inter et inter. You have certainly done the work set; that was no more than your duty. But previously you did more. You were more industrious perhaps, or at all events more interested in the subject. I am now asking for the reason of this sudden slackening of effort. You aren't ill, I suppose ? "

" No."

" Or suffering from headaches ? You do not look wonderfully well."

" Yes, I often have headaches."

" Is your everyday work too much for you then ? "

" Oh, no, not at all."

" Or are you doing too much private reading ? Be honest with me."

" No; I am reading practically nothing, Sir."

" Then I fail to understand it. There's something wrong somewhere. Will you promise me to give your work the proper attention in future ? "

Hans placed his hand in the right hand of the powerful man who looked at him with an air of grave beneficence.

" That's good, dear boy. Don't relax your effort, otherwise you will fall under the wheel."

He pressed Hans' hand and the latter walked to the door, breathing fast. He was suddenly called back.

" There's something else, Giebenrath. You see a good deal of Heilner, don't you ? "

" Yes; a fair amount."

" More than you see of any other boy, I believe, if I am not mistaken ? "

" Yes, he's my friend."

" How did that come about? You are such different temperaments."

" I can't say; at any rate he is my friend now."

" You know that I am not very fond of your friend. He is a restless, discontented spirit; he may be gifted but he does nothing and he has a bad influence on you. I would be gratified if you would avoid his company—well? "

" I can't, sir."

" You can't? And why not, I pray? "

" Because he is my friend. I can't just drop him."

" Hm. But you could extend your friendship more to other boys. You are the only one who succumbs to Heilner's bad influence and we are already seeing the consequences. What is the particular bond you have with him? "

" I don't really know myself. But we like each other and it would be cowardly of me to drop him now."

" Well, well. I am not going to compel you to. But I hope you will gradually break away from him. I should be gratified, highly gratified."

There was nothing of his earlier amiability in the Principal's final remarks. Hans was now allowed to go.

From now on he attacked his work with renewed effort. But it was no longer the light-hearted forging ahead of before; it was a painful race not to get left too far behind. He knew it was partly to do with his friendship yet he could not regard his relationship with Heilner as a loss or an obstacle; he saw in it a treasure that outweighed any loss, it was a higher, warmer life with which his former trivial and dutiful existence could not compare. It was with him as it is with young lovers; he felt capable of great and heroic deeds but not the tedious, pettifogging round of everyday. And so with a despairing sigh he assumed the yoke. It was not in his nature to imitate Heilner who worked superficially and quickly, not to say with undue haste, acquired the minimum amount of knowledge. As his friend claimed his free time every evening, he forced himself to get up an hour earlier and wrestled with his Hebrew grammar as with an enemy. At the present time only his Homer and his history gave him any pleasure. Groping his way darkly he came to an understanding of the Homeric world, and in history the heroes ceased to be names and numbers and began to approach him and look at him out of glowing eyes, and they had red lips and each one his individual face and hands—one had red, thick rough hands, one stone-like and cold, another hands that were narrow, warm and finely-veined.

Even when he was reading the scriptures in Greek he sometimes found himself surprised, even staggered by the clarity and closeness of the personalities who people them. In the sixth chapter of St. Mark, for example, where Jesus leaves the ship with his disciples and it reads:

" Straightway they knew him, they ran up to him." He would then see the Son of Man leaving the ship and recognized him at once not by his face or his physical form but by the brilliant depths of his loving eyes and a gently beckoning or inviting, welcome-bidding, bearing of his beautiful brown hand which seemed shaped and inhabited by a refined yet strong personality. The edge of a turbulent lake and the bows of a heavy fishing boat rose up for a moment and then the whole image had vanished like steaming breath in winter air.

At intervals an historical personage or event would leap from the pages of his book with the same sort of eagerness and zest as if they were longing to live again or be re-enacted and be reflected in a living eye. Hans was impressed and surprised and he felt himself profoundly and strangely transformed by these phenomena which he glimpsed as they flashed by; it was as if he had been peering through the dark earth like a glass or as if God himself had been looking at him. These precious moments came unbidden, and disappeared unlamented as if they had been pilgrims or friendly guests whom one would hesitate to accost or press to stay because they have a strange and godlike air about them.

He kept these experiences to himself and did not divulge them to Heilner. The latter's earlier melancholy had soured into cynicism which found an outlet in criticisms of school, the weather, life, the existence of God and on occasion led him to spoil for a fight or indulge in some stupid prank. As he stood apart from the rest and in opposition to them, he showed it in an attitude of defiance and hostility carrying Giebenrath, who was only too willing, along with him; so that both friends were cut off from the general crowd like an ill-omened island. But Hans gradually felt less and less disturbed by all this. If only there had not been the Principal of whom he went in secret awe. Once his favourite pupil he was now treated coldly and with an intentionally offhand manner. And he had gradually lost his enthusiasm for Hebrew, the Principal's speciality.

It was amusing to see how much the forty students—with the occasional phlegmatic exception—had changed physically and spiritually in a few months. A number of them had shot up considerably at the expense of their breadth and their wrists and ankles obtruded hopefully from clothes that had not kept pace with them. Their faces showed every possible nuance between vanishing childhood and budding but hesitant manhood, still shy of pressing its claims, boys whose bodies were not yet adultly angular had by the study of the Book of Moses acquired on their smooth brows at any rate a temporary grown-up seriousness. A pair of chubby cheeks was now a rarity.

Hans too had changed. He was now as tall and lean as Heilner and almost looked older than his friend. The smooth transparent skin of his forehead had gone and his eyes were more deeply set, his complexion was pasty, his limbs and shoulders were bony and fleshless.

The less satisfied he was with his progress in class, the more resolutely did he — under Heilner's influence — cut himself off from his companions. As he was no longer an exemplary pupil and potential top of the class and had therefore little cause to look down on them from a superior height, his aloofness ill became him. But he was unable to forgive them for making him aware of this and himself for feeling it acutely. He had frequent quarrels for example with the harmless Hartner and the boisterous Otto Wenger. When one day the latter was mocking and annoying him, Hans forgot himself and retorted with a blow. A serious fight ensued. Wenger was a coward but his weak adversary was easy game and he went for him unmercifully. Heilner was not present. The rest of the boys looked on indifferently; they were enjoying his discomfiture. He was well and truly beaten, his nose was bleeding and every rib in his body ached. All that night he could not sleep for pain and anger. He kept the incident a secret from his friend, but from this moment he resolutely avoided his Study companions and hardly exchanged a word with them.

At the beginning of the new year with the rainy afternoons and wet Sundays and long period of darkness, life in the College took a new turn. The Study, Acropolis, which had a good pianist and two flautists among its members, founded two regular musical evenings; in the

Study, Germania, they inaugurated a play-reading circle, and a few pious boys set up a Bible study circle and read a chapter of the Bible every evening in conjunction with a commentary on the Calvin Bible.

Heilner applied for membership of the play-reading circle in Germania but was refused. He seethed with fury. To spite them he went along to the Bible study group. They did not want him there either but he pushed himself in and with his insolent views and heretical allusions introduced an atmosphere of dispute and wrangling into the pious conversation of the shy little Brotherhood. He soon tired of this game but the ironic tone of his conversation still persisted. However, he now received scant attention, for the whose establishment was completely taken up by a new spirit of creative enterprise.

The person who got himself most talked about was a clever and witty member of Sparta. Apart from the question of his personal fame, he felt it incumbent on him to introduce some life into the place and provide more frequent relief from the monotony of everyday work by means of any possible diversion. His nickname was Dunstan and he discovered an original way of causing a sensation and winning a certain amount of celebrity for himself at the same time.

One morning when the boys were coming out of the dormitories they found a paper stuck on the washroom doors on which under the heading " Six epigrams from Sparta " a selection of notable personalities of the place, their foibles, rags and friendships were ridiculed in couplets. Giebenrath and Heilner did not escape attention. The little world seethed with excitement. The boys crowded at the doors as if it was a theatre entrance, and the whole mob murmured, pushed and buzzed together like a swarm of bees when their queen is about to take flight.

Next morning the door was completely covered with epigrams, Xenia, retorts, corroborations, renewed attacks in which the instigator of the whole business had been shrewd enough to take no further part. Practically every boy joined in this battle of epigrams for several days. Everybody strolled round pensively intent on a couplet, and Lucius was probably the only one who went on with his work unperturbed as ever. At length one of the masters heard of it and forbade them to continue this exciting game.

The shrewd Dunstan did not rest on his laurels; he had meantime prepared his master stroke. He chose this moment to publish the first issue of a newspaper which was hectographed in a small format on rough exercise paper; he had been collecting " copy " for weeks. It bore the title *The Porcupine* and was essentially a humorous periodical. The star feature of the first number was a humorous dialogue between the author of the Book of Joshua and a Maulbronn theological student.

It had an enormous success and Dunstan who now assumed the air and deportment of a hectically busy publisher and editor, enjoyed almost the same reputation in the establishment as the famous Aretino of old in the Venetian Republic.

General astonishment prevailed when Hermann Heilner took an enthusiastic share in the editing and together with Dunstan now supplied the enterprise with a sharp, satirical commentary for which he lacked neither the wit nor the venom. For about a month the little paper kept the whole College in a state of breathless excitement.

Giebenrath conveyed to his friend that he had neither

the wish nor the talent to participate himself. At first he hardly noticed that Heilner had of late been spending so many of his evenings in Sparta for recently he had had something else on his mind. Day after day he went about distracted and with no energy, worked slowly and without any zest and on one occasion in the Livy period he had a curious experience.

The master called on him to translate. He remained seated.

" What does this mean ? Why don't you stand up ? " the master called out angrily.

Hans did not stir. He continued to sit upright in his desk with slightly lowered head and half-closed eyes. The shout had awakened him out of a dream but the teacher's voice seemed to reach him from a very long way off. He was also conscious of his desk neighbour nudging him hard. But it seemed no concern of his. He was surrounded by other people; other hands were touching him, other voices addressing him, close, gentle, deep voices which uttered no words, only sounds like the deep murmur of a stream. And many eyes were gazing at him—strange, shining eyes, full of foreboding. Perhaps the eyes of a Roman crowd which he had just been reading about in Livy or the eyes of unknown men of whom he had dreamed or caught a glimpse in pictures.

" Giebenrath," shouted the master, " are you asleep ? "

The boy slowly opened his eyes, stared astonished at the master and shook his head.

" You've been asleep ! Can you tell me what sentence we have got to ? Well ! "

Hans indicated the place in the book; he knew very well where they were.

" Perhaps you will be good enough to stand up now ? " said the master sarcastically. And Hans stood up.

" What are you doing then ? Look at me ! "

He looked at the master. The latter was not pleased with what he saw for he shook his head in surprise.

" Are you ill, Giebenrath ? "

" No, Herr Professor."

" Sit down again and come to my study at the end of the lesson."

Hans sat down and bent over his Livy. He was fully awake and understood everything that was going on but with his inner eye he followed the many strange forms which slowly moved away to a great distance, keeping their gleaming eyes fixed on him until they faded away in a mist. At the same time the master's voice and that of the boy who was translating and all the small classroom noises came closer and closer, as real and present as ever. Desks, master's dais, blackboard stood there as usual, the large wooden compasses and set-square hung on the wall; all round sat his comrades many of whom were glancing with insolent curiosity in his direction. Then Hans was overcome with fear. " Come to my study at the end of the lesson," were the words he had heard. In the name of heaven, what had happened then ?

The master beckoned to him when the lesson was over and took him along through the rows of his staring companions.

" Now tell me what was really the matter with you. You were not asleep then ? "

" No."

" Why did you not stand up when I called you ? "

" I don't know."

" Perhaps you didn't hear me? Are you hard of hearing? "

" No. I heard you."

" And yet you didn't stand up? You had a very strange look in your eyes. What were you thinking about? "

" Nothing. I *meant* to stand up."

" Why didn't you then? Were you unwell? "

" I don't think so. I don't know what it was."

" Had you a headache? "

" No."

" Very well. Go along."

Before dinner Hans was summoned again and taken up to the Dormitory. There the Principal was waiting for him with the local doctor. The latter examined him and asked him questions but came to no very definite conclusion. The doctor laughed good-naturedly. He did not think it was serious.

" Slight nervous disorders, Principal," he smiled. " Temporary faintness—just a slight giddiness. You must see that the fellow gets some fresh air every day. I will prescribe some drops for the headaches."

From this time on Hans had to go out for an hour's fresh air every day, after dinner. He did not mind. The worst of it was that the Principal expressly forbade Heilner to join him on these walks. The latter raged and swore but it was of no avail. So Hans always went alone and derived a certain pleasure from his own company. It was the beginning of Spring. The new green ran like a clear, shallow wave over the rounded forms of the hills, the trees were losing their sharply defined brown criss-cross pattern of winter and their fresh young foliage merged into the colours of the landscape like a vast flowing tide of living green.

Earlier on, in his grammar schooldays Hans had looked at the Spring with a different eye, with a more interested curiosity in its detailed aspects. He had observed the returning birds, one species after another and the successive outbursts of blossom on the fruit-trees. Then as soon as May arrived, he had begun his fishing expeditions. But now he could not be bothered to distinguish the different species of birds or recognize the bushes by their buds. All he noticed was the general surge of life, the colours starting up everywhere; he breathed in the smell of the young leaves, smelt the milder, intoxicating air and walked through the fields full of wonder. He tired easily and felt a continual desire to lie down and fall asleep. Almost all the time he saw other things than those that actually surrounded him. What they were he did not know himself and he did not give any thought to the matter. They were distinct, unusual, affecting visions which stood round him like frozen portraits or avenues of exotic trees, but nothing appeared to happen among them. Untroubled portraits to contemplate, but this very act of contemplation was also an experience. It was like being transported to another world and among other men. It was a journey on to strange soil, a soft, agreeable soil to tread and a strange air blew, full of well-being and dreamy fragrance. Sometimes these images were replaced by a feeling, dark, warm and moving as if a gentle hand was caressing his body.

Hans found it a struggle to concentrate both in his reading and his other work. The subjects that failed to hold his interest were as elusive as shadows and if he wanted to remember the Hebrew vocabulary for the lesson, he had to learn it up at the last minute. But the moments of vision when he suddenly was in the bodily presence of everything

114

that had been described in his reading seemed more alive, indeed much more real than the actual objects that surrounded him. And while he noticed with despair that his memory seemed unable to take any more in and became poorer and more uncertain every day, sometimes memories from earlier days came upon him with a strange clarity, both odd and disturbing. He would frequently find himself thinking about his father or old Anna in the middle of a lesson or while he was reading, or one of his former teachers or schoolfellows would appear as it were in the flesh before him and for the time being monopolized his attention. He re-lived scenes from his stay in Stuttgart, the *Landexamen* period and the holidays that followed or saw himself sitting by the river with his fishing-rod, smelt the smell of the sunlit water; and yet he had the feeling that the time of which he was dreaming was long years back in the past.

One somewhat damp, dark evening he was pacing up and down with Heilner, chatting about his father, fishing and school. His friend was noticeably quiet, let him speak, gave a nod now and again or made a few thoughtful passes in the air with his small ruler with which he toyed all the day. Gradually Hans too fell silent; it had grown quite dark and they sat down on a window sill.

" I say, Hans," Heilner began finally. His voice was excited and unsteady.

" What ? "

" Oh nothing."

" Do go on ! "

" I was just thinking—since you talked to me about all sorts of things . . ."

" Well ? "

" Tell me, Hans, haven't you ever run after a girl ? "

A silence followed. It was a subject that neither of them had mentioned before. Hans shied off it, although that enigmatic territory held for him the fascination of an enchanted garden. He felt himself blush and his fingers trembled.

"Only once," he whispered. "I was just a silly child then."

Another pause.

". . . And you, Heilner?"

Heilner sighed.

"Oh, don't; it's no use talking about it you know. It doesn't do any good."

"Do go on!"

"I, I've got a sweetheart."

"You? Is it true?"

"Back at home. A neighbour. And I kissed her this winter."

"Kissed her?"

"Yes. It was dark. I was helping her to remove her skates on the ice in the evening, and I gave her a kiss."

"Did she say anything?"

"Not a word. She just ran off."

"And then?"

"And then! . . . Nothing."

He sighed again and gazed at him as if he was a hero who had returned from a forbidden garden.

Then the bell rang and they had to go to bed. When the lamp had been extinguished and everything had become quiet, Hans lay there for more than an hour, thinking about the kiss which Heilner had given his sweetheart.

The next day he wanted to ask him more about it but he felt awkward and his friend was too shy to return to the subject as Hans had not inquired further.

Things in school were getting worse and worse for Hans. The masters were beginning to frown and look oddly at him; the Principal was grim and annoyed; even Hans' companions had long been aware that Giebenrath was slipping from his pedestal and had ceased to aim at being first in class. Heilner alone failed to notice anything — school affairs were not important to him—and Hans saw it all happening and changing without paying it any attention.

Meantime Heilner had had enough of newspaper editing and turned to his friend again. In defiance of the ban, he accompanied Hans several times on his daily walks, lay beside him in the sun day-dreaming, read poetry, made jokes at the expense of the Principal. Every day Hans was hoping to hear more revelations from Heilner about his romantic love affair, yet the longer he put off asking the more difficult he found it to bring himself to do so. Both the boys were as unpopular as ever among their comrades, for Heilner's malicious gibes in *The Porcupine* had won him no one's confidence.

By this time the paper was beginning to peter out in any case; it had gone on too long; the editors had only intended it to fill in the tedious weeks between winter and spring. Now the new season of the year had plenty to offer in the way of botanising, walks, open-air sports. Every afternoon, gymnasts, boxers, runners and players of ball games filled the cloister garden with their shouts and activity.

And there was an additional sensation of which once more Hermann Heilner was the originator and storm-centre.

It had come to the Principal's ears that Heilner had defied his prohibition and was accompanying Giebenrath on his walks almost every day. On this occasion the Principal did not worry Giebenrath and was content to summon the chief culprit, his old enemy, to his study. He addressed him with a friendly familiarity which made Heilner curl up immediately. He reproached him with his disobedience. Heilner explained that he was Giebenrath's friend and that no one had the right to come between them. He made an ugly scene as the result of which he was kept in for several hours and strictly forbidden to go out with Giebenrath in the future.

So Hans embarked next day on his official walk alone. He came back at two o'clock in the afternoon and joined the other boys in the classroom. At the beginning of the lesson it transpired that Heilner was absent. It was very much a repetition of the previous occasion when Hindu had disappeared, only this time no one supposed that it was merely a matter of lateness. At three o'clock the whole college went out with three of the teachers to search for the missing boy. They split up into groups, ran through the woods shouting for him. Many of the boys and even two of the teachers did not rule out the possibility that he had done himself mischief.

At five o'clock they telegraphed to all the police stations and in the evening an express-letter was posted to Heilner's father. By late evening there was no trace of the boy and whispering could be heard in the dormitories well into the night. The most widely accepted theory among the boys was that he had thrown himself into the water. Others thought he had just run away home. But it had been discovered that he had no money on him.

They looked at Hans as though he was bound to know all about it. But it was not so; in point of fact he was the most worried and frightened of them all and at night in the dormitory when he heard the others asking questions, producing theories and joking about it, he buried himself under his blankets and endured long hours of torment as he lay there distressed about his friend. A premonition that he would never come back seized hold of his panic-stricken heart and filled him with dread, until at length. worn out with anxiety he fell asleep.

At that same moment Heilner lay only a few miles away in a wood. He was too chilled to sleep but he drew deep breaths enjoying his freedom and stretched his limbs as if he had escaped from a narrow cage. He had been on the go since midday, had bought a loaf of bread in Knittlingen and now and again took a bite from it as he gazed through the spring branches still only lightly clad with leaves at the darkness, the stars and chasing clouds. Where he would finally land up was a matter of indifference to him; at least he had escaped from the loathsome college and had shown the Principal that his will was stronger than all his orders and prohibitions.

All next day they continued the vain search. He spent the second night near a village among heaps of straw in a field; in the morning he went back into the forest and only towards evening when he wanted to go into a village did he fall into the hands of a policeman. With an air of scornful amusement the latter took him along to the Town Hall where Heilner won the sympathy of the mayor with his jokes and smooth tongue and was invited to spend the night at his house and supped generously on ham and eggs. The following day his father, who had come over, collected him.

Excitement ran high in the College when the fugitive was brought back. But he held his head erect and appeared in no way to regret his brilliant escapade. He was expected to apologize but he refused, and displayed neither timidity nor subservience before the teachers' tribunal. They had hoped to keep him but the cup was now full. He was expelled in disgrace and that same evening left the college for good with his father. His leave-taking from his friend Hans Giebenrath, had to be confined to a handshake.

The Principal made a magnificently impressive speech about this scandalous case of insubordination and decadence. His report to the authorities at Stuttgart was couched in feebler, more factual and measured terms. All future correspondence with the expelled monster was forbidden, which merely caused Hans Giebenrath to smile. For weeks Heilner and his flight was the all-absorbing topic. Distance and time had modified the general view about him and many now regarded the fugitive whom they once so nervously avoided as an eagle soaring from his cage.

Hellas now had two empty desks and the last occupant was not so quickly forgotten as the first. It would indeed have suited the Principal better if he could have felt the second was being as quietly cared for as his predecessor. But Heilner took no steps to disturb the peace of the establishment. His friend waited and waited but no letter came. He had vanished and gone; memories of his physical shape and his flight from the school became first past history and then gradually turned into legend. After many further brilliant escapades and vagaries of fortune the boy was finally reduced to order by the grim realities of life which made if not a hero at any rate a man of him.

The suspicion that rested on Hans who was left behind, of having previous knowledge about Heilner's flight robbed him completely of the teachers' good opinion. When during the course of a lesson he had given a wrong answer to several questions, one of them remarked "Why didn't you go off with that fine friend of yours?"

The Principal let him go on sitting there, eyeing him narrowly with the same derisive pity with which the Pharisee regarded the publican. This Giebenrath was no longer one of them; he was a leper.

CHAPTER FIVE

Like a hamster with its laid-in store, Hans gained a brief respite by virtue of his previously acquired knowledge. Then followed a painful period of starvation, interrupted by short ineffectual attempts—at the hopelessness of which he was wryly amused—to save the situation. He now ceased to torment himself to no purpose, threw his Homer after the Pentateuch and the algebra book after his Xenophon and without becoming unduly perturbed watched his good reputation sink step by step in his teachers' eye from good to fair, from fair to satisfactory, from satisfactory to unsatisfactory. When he was free from his headache which was not often, he thought of Hermann Heilner, dreamed his idle, wistful dreams and spent whole hours sunk in vague thoughts. His reply to renewed reproaches of all the teachers was a good-natured, deprecatory smile. Wiedrich, a friendly assistant teacher, was the only one who was distressed by this desperate smile and he treated this boy who had lost his way with sympathetic forbearance. The rest of the staff were merely indignant and treated Hans with contemptuous neglect or made occasional attempts to arouse his slumbering ambition with sarcastic gibes. " In case you happen not to be asleep, might I trouble you to read this sentence ? "

The Principal was righteously indignant. This vain man had great ideas about the power of his glance and was beside himself with rage when Giebenrath repeatedly faced his majestically threatening brows with the humble, deprecatory smile which gradually got on his nerves.

" Don't give that meaningless smile. You have got good cause to weep rather."

A horrified letter from his father begging him to improve made a deeper impression on him. The Principal had written to Herr Giebenrath and the latter was very perturbed. His letter to Hans was a collection of all the encouragement and suitable formulas of indignation at that worthy man's command but an unconscious note of plaintive misery came through which his son found distressing.

All these devoted leaders of youth, from the Principal down to Herr Giebenrath, including senior and junior assistant masters, saw in Hans an obstacle to their wishes, something resistant and lazy that must somehow be forced back into the fold. Not one—with the possible exception of the sympathetic Wiedrich—could penetrate the desperate smile on the boy's small face to the foundering spirit within, suffering and looking about him in terror and despair as he sank. Nor did it occur to any of them that the school and the ruthless ambition of a father and some of teachers had reduced this fragile creature to such a state. Why had he had to work late into the night during the most sensitive and critical years of his boyhood ? Why had they taken his rabbits away from him, intentionally estranged him from his friends at the grammar school, forbidden him to go fishing and wander around, preferring to instil into him the empty and commonplace ideal of a wretched and gnawing ambition. Why, even after the Examination had they not allowed him to enjoy the well-deserved holidays ?

Now the overworked little steed lay by the roadside and was of no more use to anyone.

Towards the beginning of the summer the State doctor

explained once again that it was a question of a nervous condition, mainly due to growing. Hans was to look after himself well in the holidays, have plenty to eat, spend plenty of time in the woods; then he would soon recover.

Unfortunately it never got as far as that. There were still three weeks to go before the holidays when Hans received a severe reproof from one of the senior masters during an afternoon lesson. While the teacher was still rating him, Hans sank back into his desk and began to tremble uncontrollably and then burst into a prolonged fit of weeping which interrupted the whole lesson. He spent the remainder of the day in bed.

The following day in the mathematics lesson he was asked to draw a geometric figure on the blackboard and go through the proof orally. He stood up but as he faced the blackboard he was overcome with dizziness; he took the chalk and ruler and made meaningless scrawls on the board, then dropped them and when he stooped down to pick them up, stayed kneeling on the floor, unable to rise to his feet.

The State doctor was somewhat put out that his patient should indulge in such exhibitions. He ventured a cautious opinion, prescribed immediate sick-leave and recommended calling in a nerve specialist.

"He's contracting St. Vitus' dance," he whispered to the Principal who nodded his head and found it expedient to change the ungracious expression of anger on his face into one of paternal sympathy which he found no difficulty in doing and which became him well.

He and the doctor composed a letter to Herr Giebenrath, put it in the boy's pocket and packed him off home. The Principal's anger had turned into deep apprehension— what would the educational authorities, already disturbed by the Heilner case, think about this new misfortune? To the general astonishment of the school he dispensed with a lecture suitable to the occasion and treated Hans with an unwonted consideration during these last hours. It was obvious to him that the boy would not return from his sick-leave—even in the event of his recovery. As he had already lost ground, he could not possibly make up the months or even weeks of lost time. He took leave of the boy with an encouragingly hearty " auf Wiedersehen " but every time he entered Hellas in the next few days and saw the three empty desks, he felt disturbed and found it difficult to suppress the thought that perhaps a portion of the blame for the disappearance of two talented pupils might be attached to him. But being a bold and healthy man he managed to dismiss these gloomy and futile doubts from his mind.

The monastery with its churches, gateway, gables and towers sank behind the young student as he departed carrying his small valise; the forest and hill ranges vanished and in their place arose the fertile meadow orchards of the Badenese borderland; then came Pforzheim and immediately behind began the blue-black pine trees of the Black Forest, intersected by numerous river valleys, looking bluer, cooler and holding more promise of shade than ever in this hot summer haze. The boy contemplated the changing and increasingly familiar landscape not without pleasure, until, as he drew near his home town, he remembered his father, and a painful anxiety about the reception he would have more or less ruined any pleasure of this journey back. The journey to Stuttgart for the examination and his first arrival at Maubronn with the mixture of joy and anxiety came back into his mind. What use had it all been ? He knew as well as the Principal that he would never be returning; it meant an end to training college, study and every ambitious hope. Yet the thought did not sadden him, only his fear of his disappointed father whose hopes he had betrayed weighed heavily on his heart. But for the present he had no other wish after all the torture he had been through than to rest, have a long sleep and a good cry, and to be left in peace to dream to his heart's content. He was afraid he would not be able to do this at home with his father. By the end of the railway journey he had a violent headache, and stopped looking out of the window although they were now passing through his favourite part of the world among whose woods and hills he had formerly rambled with such pleasure; and he almost failed to get out at his home station.

Now he stood there with his umbrella and valise while his father surveyed him. The Principal's last report had changed his disappointment and indignation with his failure of a son into a kind of baffled fear. He had pictured Hans in a state of collapse, and thin and weak though he now found him, he did not look exactly unhealthy and after all was still walking on his own legs. That was some comfort at any rate. The worst thing was his secret dread of the nervous breakdown which the doctor and Principal had written to him about. Hitherto no member of his family had ever suffered from any nervous disorder; they had always spoken of such illnesses with unsympathetic mockery in the way they talked about lunatics, and now his own Hans was coming home suffering from something of the same kind.

On his first day home Hans was glad to be spared any reproaches. Then he became aware of the timid, awkward consideration with which his father was treating him and which was such an obvious effort on his part. At times he realized too that his father was examining him with strangely probing looks and curiosity, speaking to him in a subdued, unnatural tone and watching him, under the illusion that his son did not notice it. The result was to make him more frightened than ever and a vague fear about his state began to torment him.

When the weather was fine he lay outside in the forest for hours on end and felt better. A faint echo of his childhood's joys filled his damaged spirit; his pleasure in flowers and insects, in observing birds or tracking animals. But it was short-lived. He mostly lazed in the moss suffering from headaches, and he would vainly try to think of something until his day-dreaming took over and transported him to other spheres.

Once he had the following dream. He saw his friend Hermann Heilner lying dead on a bier and wanted to go to him but the Principal and the staff restrained him and drove him back with blows every time he pressed forward. Not only the masters from the Training College and junior assistants were present but his old Headmaster and the Stuttgart examiners, all with sneering expressions on their faces. Suddenly the scene shifted elsewhere; the drowned Hindu lay on the bier and his grotesque father with the top hat stood by, bow-legged and sorrowful.

Then another dream. He was running in the forest, searching for the runaway Heilner and he kept seeing him disappear in the distance among the tree-trunks whenever he wanted to call out to him. At length Heilner stood still, allowed him to approach and said " I say, I have a sweetheart." Then he laughed uproariously and vanished into the undergrowth.

He saw a slender, handsome man with quiet, godlike eyes and beautiful, gentle hands step out of a boat, and he ran towards him. But it suddenly came to a stop and Hans racked his brain to think what it was all about until the passage in the Scriptures came back to him, εὐθὺς ἐπιγνόντες αὐτὸν περιέδραμον —immediately when they recognised him, they went up to him—

And now he had to think what conjugation form περιέδραμον was and how the Present tense, the Infinitive, Perfect, Future of the verb went; he had to conjugate it in the singular and plural, and he got into a fever and panic as soon as he was stuck. When he came to himself again, his head seemed to hurt all over inside, and when his face was involuntarily distorted into his old smile of resignation and guilt, he seemed to hear the Principal saying, " What stupid kind of grin is that ? Do you need to grin as well ! "

In short, despite some isolated days when he felt better, Hans' condition showed no improvement; rather the contrary. The family doctor who had attended his mother in the past and had signed her death certificate after her last illness, and treated his father who often suffered slight attacks of gout, pulled a long face and put off expressing an opinion from one day to the next.

It was only in these weeks that Hans realized that he had no friends from his last two years at the grammar school. Some of the friends of that period had left the town, others he now saw going about as apprentices and he had no bond, or anything in common with them, and none of them cared about him. On two occasions the Headmaster addressed a few friendly words to him, the Latin master and the vicar also nodded amicably at him in the street, but Hans was no longer any concern of theirs. He had ceased to be a vessel into which all manner of things could be stuffed, a field to be sown with a variety of seeds: it was no longer rewarding to spend time and trouble on him.

It might have helped if the vicar had shown a little interest in the boy. But what could he do? What he could supply, knowledge or at the least the desire for it, he had not withheld from the boy at the time when it was wanted and more than that it was not his to impart. He was not one of those parsons about whose Latin one has doubts and whose sermons are taken from well-known sources but to whom one is glad to turn in bad times because they have a sympathetic glance and a friendly word for every-body's troubles. Nor was Herr Giebenrath a friend or comforter though he tried hard to hide his bitter disappointment over Hans.

So the boy felt himself abandoned and unloved and sat about in the small garden in the sun or lay down in the woods and gave himself up to his dreams or tormenting thoughts. He was unable to take refuge in reading without bringing on pains in his head and eyes because, whenever he opened any of his old books the ghost of his training college days and all its worries rose up before him, haunted him with joyless and intimidating dreams and stared at him with burning eyes.

In his present desperate and forlorn condition another ghost approached in the guise of a treacherous comforter and gradually became an indispensable familiar—it was the thought of death. It was easy enough to procure a firearm or contrive a slip-knot on a tree somewhere in the forest. Such thoughts accompanied him almost daily on his walks and he inspected quiet and lonely spots and finally found one where it would be pleasant to die and decided definitely to make his end there. He paid it frequent visits, sat down and derived a strange pleasure from the thought that they would soon be finding his body lying there dead. The branch for the rope was chosen and tested for strength and no further difficulties stood in the way. Little by little, between long intervals, he composed a brief letter to his father and a very long one to Herman Heilner which were to be discovered on his body.

These preparations and the sense of security his decision gave him exercised a beneficent influence on his mood. He spent hours sitting under the fateful branch during which the feeling of oppression lifted and was replaced by one almost of well-being.

He did not really know why he had not hanged himself from the branch long ago. The resolve had been made, his death was decided on, and sometimes he felt quite well and latterly he had not scorned to enjoy the lovely sunshine or indulge in day-dreams in the way one does before setting off on a long voyage. He could make a start any day; everything was in order and there was a special kind of rueful pleasure about lingering for a while among the old surroundings, and looking into the faces of the people who had no idea of his dangerous resolutions. Every time he met the doctor he could not help thinking, " now you shall see."

Fate allowed him to rejoice in his dark intentions and watched him enjoy a few drops of pleasure and zest from the cup of death. Fate might indeed be indifferent to this mutilated young life but it must be allowed to complete its cycle and must not leave the arena until it had tasted the bitter sweet of life for a little while longer.

The old haunting and tormenting imaginings occurred less frequently; they gave way to a weary indifference, a painless, indolent mood during which Hans distractedly watched the days and hours go by, gazed calmly at the blue sky and seemed at times to be walking in his sleep or to have taken refuge in his childhood days. On one occasion he was sitting under the pine-tree in the garden at dusk, unconsciously humming an old jingle which had come back to him from his grammar school days

> " Alas, I am so weary
> Alas I am so worn
> I have no money in my purse
> And I am so forlorn."

He hummed it to the old tune without realizing that he had now repeated it for the twentieth time. However his father was standing by the window, listening, thoroughly frightened. This stupid, nonsensical sing-song was utterly incomprehensible to his unimaginative nature and with a sigh he attributed it to a hopeless softening of the brain. From this time on he watched the boy with increasing anxiety. Hans noticed it and was distressed but still he could not bring himself to take the rope and make use of it on the strong branch he had selected.

Meantime the hot days of summer had arrived and a year had already gone by since the Landexamen and the summer holidays that followed. Sometimes Hans thought back to it all without any particular emotion; indeed his feelings had become somewhat numbed. He would have loved to have begun his fishing again but he dared not ask his father. He felt tortured every time he stood by the water and he frequently lingered by the bank where nobody saw him and with eager eyes followed the movements of the dark, silent fish as they swam about. With the approach of evening he would walk for some distance upstream to the bathing place, and as he had to keep passing Inspector

Gessler's little house, he chanced to discover that Emma Gessler with whom he had been infatuated three years ago was now back home again. He looked at her inquisitively once or twice but he thought her less attractive than before. She had been a slender-limbed, neatly-built slip of a girl; now she had grown up, her movements were heavier and she had her hair dressed in modern, adult style which completely changed her appearance. Nor did her long dresses suit her and her attempts to look the lady were decidedly infelicitous. To Hans she seemed like a joke but at the same time he felt distressed as he remembered the oddly mysterious glow of warmth he had experienced in the old days whenever he set eyes on her. But in those days it had all been different, so much nicer, gayer and more lively ! For so long now his experience had been confined to Latin, history, Greek, examinations, the seminary and headaches. In the old days there had been books of fairy-tales, stories of robber-bands, he had constructed a home-made hammer mill and in the evenings he had listened to Liese's adventure stories in the Naschold gateway; in those days he had for some time looked on old neighbour Gross-johann, nicknamed Garibaldi, as a murderous thief and had nightmares about him, and all through the year there had been something to look forward to each month— hay-making, harvesting the clover, then the beginning of the fishing season or crayfish catching and hop-picking, shaking down the plums, potato-fires, the start of the threshing and between times and still more, each welcome Sunday and feast-day. There had been a whole host of things which attracted him with their secret magic—houses, narrow streets, hay-lofts, fountains, hedges, human beings and animals of every kind had been either familiar and beloved or mysteriously fascinating. He had helped with the hop-picking and listened as the peasant girls had sung and had been struck by certain verses in their songs most of which were grotesquely comic but others so full of pathos that he felt a lump in his throat as he listened.

But it had all faded away and come to an end without his noticing it. First the evenings at Liese's had stopped then the minnow-fishing on Sunday mornings, then the fairy-tale readings, and thus, one thing after another up to the hop-picking and the hammer mill in the garden. Where had all those days gone?

And so the precocious boy was now experiencing an unreal new childhood in these days of his illness. The mood that harked back to childhood now flowed back with a sudden outburst of longing into those wonderful, twilight years and he wandered spellbound in a forest of memories whose strength and clearness was possibly the result of his illness. He experienced it all with no less warmth and passion than he had in the reality before; his betrayed and violated childhood surged up in him like a long pent-up spring.

When a tree is pollarded, it puts out new shoots at the base, and in the same way a soul too which was ruined in the bud, finds its way back to the springtime of beginnings and prescient childhood as if it might discover new hopes there and tie up the broken threads once again. The roots thrive quickly, full of sap, but it is only a semblance of life and never again will it became a healthy tree.

That was how it was with Hans Giebenrath and so we must therefore accompany him a short way on his dreams in the land of childhood.

The Giebenrath house stood close by the old stone bridge and formed the angle between two very different streets. One, — to which the house was considered to belong—was the longest, broadest and best in the town and was called Gerbergasse. The other led steeply uphill, was short, narrow and dismal and was called "Zum Falken" after an ancient, long-disappeared hostelry which had borne the sign of a falcon.

Every house in the Gerberstrasse was inhabited by good, solid citizens, people who owned their houses, had their own family vaults and gardens which rose steeply behind in terraces and the fences of which, erected in the sixties, bordered the railway embankment which was overgrown with yellow broom. The sole rival to the Gerbergasse in the matter of superior buildings was the Market-place where church, Council Chamber, Law-court, Townhall and vicarage with their unblemished respectability gave a noble impression of civic pride. The Gerberstrasse did not indeed possess any official buildings but there were old and new middle-class residences with impressive entrances, small, pretty, half-timbered houses, bright attractive gables; and it owed its friendly, comfortable aspect to the fact that it consisted of a single row of houses, for on the other side of the street, at the foot of a wall provided with supporting piles, ran the river.

If the Gerberstrasse was long, broad, light, spacious and elegant, the "Falken" was the very opposite. Here stood dingy, tumbledown houses covered with crumbly plaster, houses with overhanging gables, doors and windows that had frequently collapsed and been repaired, twisted chimney stacks and damaged gutterings. The houses robbed each other of light and space and the street was narrow and fantastically tortuous and shrouded moreover in an eternal twilight which turned into damp darkness in rainy weather or when the sun had gone down. Lots of washing hung perpetually from poles and lines for the alley was small and poor and contained a great many families not to mention all the sub-tenants and those that dossed there for the night. Every corner of the tumbledown houses was crowded; it was a nest of poverty, vice and disease. When typhoid broke out, it was there that it started, likewise if a murder was committed, and if there was a burglary the " Falken " was the first place to undergo a search. Hawkers lodged there, including the comic vendor of cleaning powder, Hottehotte, and the scissor-grinder Adam Hittel, and to him all manner of crime and vice was attributed.

During his early school years Hans had been a frequent guest in the " Falken." In the company of a dubious gang of ragged, flaxen-haired boys he had listened to murder-stories as recounted by the notorious Lotte Frohmüller. She was the divorced wife of a small innkeeper and had spent five years of her life in prison. In her time she had been a well-known belle, had had a great number of lovers among the factory hands and had been the cause of even more scandals and stabbing incidents. Now she lived alone and spent her evenings after the factories had closed, boiling coffee and telling yarns. At such times her door stood wide open and in addition to the women and young workers, a crowd of neighbours and children continually listened to her in fascinated horror from the doorstep. The water boiled in the kettle on the black stone hearth, a tallow candle burned near it and with the blue flames from the small coal fire lit the dark, crowded room with weird flickerings that projected the shadows of the spectators on the walls and ceiling in monstrous shapes, endowing them with ghostly movements.

It was here that the eight-year-old boy made the acquaintance of the Finkenbein brothers and kept up a friendship with them for about a year in defiance of a strict injunction on the part of his father. They were called Dolf and Emil and had the most doubtful reputation of any of the town urchins; they were famed for orchard-robberies, minor poaching offences in the woods and as perpetrators of endless mischief of one sort and another. They also trafficked in birds-eggs, lead bullets, young ravens, starlings and hares, laid illegal night-lines and were thoroughly at home in all the town-gardens for no fence had sufficient spikes, no wall was thickly enough encrusted with broken glass to prevent them climbing over without any difficulty.

And then there was above all Hermann Rechtenheil who lived in the "Falken" and with whom Hans had become very intimate. He was an orphan and a sickly precocious, unusual child. Because one of his legs was shorter than the other, he had to go about with a stick, and was unable to take part in the street games. He was slightly built and had a pale, intense face that ended in a pointed chin. He was exceptionally gifted in anything involving manual dexterity, had a passion for fishing with which he infected Hans. At that time Hans did not hold a licence but this did not prevent them from fishing; this they did from various hidden spots for if sport may be described as a pleasure, poaching has, as everybody knows, a thrill of its own. The lame Rechtenheil taught Hans how to cut good fishing rods, how to plait horsehair, how to dye lines, how to twist running knots, how to sharpen fish-hooks. He taught him to study the weather, examine the water, cloud it with bran, choose the right bait and attach it effectively; he taught him how to distinguish the different kinds of fish, how to watch the fish and keep the line at the right depth.

By his mere presence and example he silently communicated the holds and the subtle instinct for the moment when to wind in or let out. He had nothing but scorn for the handsome rods, floats, gut lines and all artificially manufactured paraphernalia and convinced Hans that you could not possibly fish successfully unless every individual part of your tackle was home-made and you had also put the whole thing together yourself.

A quarrel had caused the Finkenbein brothers to break with Hans but it was not through a difference of opinion that the quiet, lame Rechtenheil left him. He had merely stretched himself one February day on his pathetic little bed, laid his crutch on his clothes on a chair, become feverish and quickly and quietly died. The " Falken " forgot him immediately and Hans alone kept a happy memory of him.

But this no means exhausted the number of unusual residents in the " Falken ". Everybody knew the Postman, Rotteler, who had been dismissed for drunkenness and who lay dead drunk regularly once a fortnight in the gutter or was involved in scandals at night, but who for the rest of the time was like a well-behaved child and smiled benevolently at everyone, always bubbling over with friendliness. He let Hans help himself from his oval snuff-box, occasionally accepted fish from him, roasted them in butter and invited Hans to share the dinner. He possessed a stuffed buzzard with glass eyes and an old chiming-clock which played old fashioned dance melodies in thin delicate tones. And who did not know the aged mechanic, Porsch, who still wore cuffs even when he was walking about barefoot ? As the son of a strict board-school teacher of the old type, he knew by heart half the Bible as well as endless proverbs and aphorisms, but neither this fact nor his snow-white hair prevented him from cutting a dash with all the women and frequently getting drunk. When he was drunk, he enjoyed sitting on the curbstone at the corner of the Giebenrath house, calling to all the passers-by by name and serving up a rich supply of aphorisms.

"Hans Giebenrath junior, my dear son, listen to what I say! What saith Ecclesiasticus? ' Blessed is the man that hath not slipped with his mouth and whose conscience hath not condemned him. As of the green leaves on a thick tree, some fall and some grow; so is the generation of flesh and blood, one cometh to an end, and another is born.' Well, now you can go home, you young rascal."

Despite all these pious utterances, old Porsch was full of sinister, legendary tales of ghosts and suchlike. He knew the spots they haunted and he wavered between belief and disbelief in his own stories. He usually began them in doubting tones, boastful yet self deprecatory as if he was making fun of the story and his listeners but gradually, as the narration continued he crouched down nervously, lowered his voice more and more and ended in a quiet, penetrating, uncanny whisper.

What dark, haunting and uncanny mysteries this wretched little street harboured!

In it too, after his business had collapsed and his neglected shop was completely ruined, the locksmith Brendle had lived. He sat half the day at his little window, looking grimly at the animated street, and sometimes when one of the unruly unwashed children from the neighbouring houses had fallen into his hands, he had tortured it with malicious glee, tweaked its ears, pulled its hair and pinched it black and blue. One day, however, he was found hanged above his staircase; he looked so horrible that no one dared approach his body until the old mechanic Porsch cut the wire with metal shears from behind, whereupon the body with its protruding tongue, plunged forward and thumped down the stairs into the midst of the terrified spectators.

Every time Hans left the broad, bright Gerbergasse for the dark and humid "Falken" he was overcome by the strange, stuffy air, an exciting sense of oppressiveness, a mixture of curiosity, fear, bad conscience and delicious foreboding. The "Falken" was the one spot where a fairy tale, a miracle, a dreadful horror could happen, where any magic was credible, where it was possible to believe in ghosts and where you could feel the same thrilling shudder that you felt as you read old legends and the horrific Reutlinger Folk Tales which the teachers confiscated, and recounted the wicked deeds and punishments of "penny blood" villains like the Sonnenwirtles, Schinderhanns, Postmichels, Jack the Rippers and other sinister heroes, criminals and adventurers.

Apart from the "Falken" there was one other place which was different from anywhere else and where you could hear and experience things and lose yourself in dark lofts and strange rooms. It was the large nearby tannery, the huge old house where the big animal hides hung in dimly lit lofts, where there were hidden cavities and barred passages in the cellar and where in the evening Liese told her wonderful tales to all the children. It was quieter, more friendly and more human than in the "Falken" but just as mysterious. The activities of the tanners in the various chambers, the cellar yard and on the floors were weird and peculiar, the vast, yawning rooms were as quiet as they were intriguing, the powerfully built and surly master was shunned and dreaded as an ogre, and

Liese went about the remarkable house like a fairy protector and mother to all the children, birds, cats and puppies, brimful of kindness, stories and ballad songs.

Hans' thoughts and dreams now moved in this world to which he had been so long a stranger. He sought refuge from his great disappointment and despair in the good days of the past when he had still cherished hopes and had seen the world standing before him like a vast magic forest that concealed grim dangers, treasures that bore a curse and castles of shining emerald in its impenetrable depths. He had made a little way into this wilderness then he had become tired before anything miraculous had happened, and now he stood once more by the mysterious entrance, this time excluded but still attracted thither by idle curiosity.

Hans revisited the " Falken " a few times. He found the familiar dinginess and evil smell, the old corners and ill-lit staircases; grey-haired men and women still sat in front of the doors and unwashed, fair-haired children ran round yelling. Porsch, the mechanic had aged, failed to recognize Hans and gave a scornful bleat by way of reply to his shy greeting. Grossjohann, nicknamed Garibaldi, likewise Lotte Frohmüller had died. Rötteler, the ex-postman, was still there. He complained that the boys had broken his chiming-clock, offered Hans his snuff-box and then tried to beg money off him. Finally he reported that one of the Finkenbeins now worked in the cigar factory and already drank like a fish; the other had disappeared after a fight with knives at a church fair and had been missing for a year. It all seemed very sordid and depressing to Hans.

And one evening he went over to the tannery. He felt drawn there, through the gateway and across the damp tannery yard as if his childhood lay hidden in the large old house with its vanished joys.

Up the twisting staircase and across the hall, he came to the dark staircase, groped his way through to the loft where the animal hides were hanging up and as he inhaled the acrid smell of leather, he was assaulted by a sudden host of memories. He climbed down again and returned to the yard where the tannery pits and narrow roofed, high frames stood for drying the pieces of pressed tan bark. Liese was sitting as he might have expected on a bench by the wall, had a basket of potatoes for peeling before her and a bunch of eager children listening to her as she told stories.

Hans stood in the dark doorway and peeped in. It was dusk and the tannery-yard was filled with a great peace; except for the faint murmur of the river that flowed behind the wall all you could hear was Liese's knife scraping the potatoes and her voice as she retailed her stories. The children squatted quietly round her and hardly moved. She was telling the legend of St. Christopher; how one night he had heard a child's voice calling out across the river.

Hans listened for a while, then walked across the dark hall and back home. He knew now that he could never be a child again and sit at Liese's feet in the tannery yard, and from this time on he avoided the tannery as well as the " Falken."

CHAPTER SIX

It was getting well into autumn. Isolated deciduous trees
glowed yellow and red like torches among the pine forests,
the valleys were already filled with heavy mist, and vapour
rose off the river in the cold morning air.

The pale ex-student strolled round in the open air every
day, joyless and weary, avoiding even the few opportunities
of social intercourse that were offered. The doctor
prescribed drops, cod-liver oil, eggs and cold shower
baths.

It was not surprising that none of these things were any
help. Every healthy life must have an aim and a content;
young Giebenrath had lost both. His father had now
determined to let him become either a clerk or learn a
trade. The boy was still weak and needed to recruit his
strength to some extent, but they would soon be able to
think over the question and discuss it with him seriously.

Ever since his first confused reactions had been allayed
and he had ceased thinking about suicide, Hans had left
the excitable and intermittent moods of anxiety for a
uniform melancholy into which he sank slowly and
defencelessly as it were into a soft, muddy bottom.

Now he roamed the autumn meadows and succumbed to
the influence of the season. The decline of the year, the
silent fall of the leaves, the russet-coloured fields, the thick
early morning mists, the ripe, tired dying of the vegetation
drove him, as it does all sick people, into heavy, hopeless
moods and thoughts of deep sadness. He felt the desire to
wither with it, fall asleep and die too; and he felt it all the

more in that it ran counter to all his youthful instincts which clung to life with quiet obstinacy.

He watched the trees turning yellow, brown and finally lose their leaves, saw the milk white mist rising like smoke from the woods, and the gardens in which life was dying after the last fruits had been gathered, and people no longer looked at the fading asters—and the river in which bathing and fishing had come to an end and the surface of which was covered with withered leaves and the frosty towpath deserted except for a few hardy tanners. For some days he had been collecting up masses of apple pulp, for they were all busy now with the cider making in the pressing sheds and all the mills, and in the town the scent of the new juice, faintly intoxicating, swept down all the streets.

In the lower mill Flaig, the shoemaker, had rented a small press and had invited Hans to the cider harvest.

On the square before the mill stood large and small presses, carts, baskets, sacks full of fruit, tubs, vats and barrels, whole mountains of pulp, wooden levers, wheel-barrows and other empty vehicles. The presses were active, and gave off a series of creaks, moans and crunching noises. Most of them were green lacquered and the green with the yellow-brown of the pulp, the colour of the apple-baskets, the bright green river, the barefoot children and the clear autumn sunlight gave an impression of joy, zest for life and plenty to all the onlookers. The crunching up of the apples was a rough and appetizing sound. No one who strolled up and heard it could resist seizing hold of an apple and biting at it. The juice, fresh and sweet, flowed from the nozzle in a thick, reddish-yellow stream, laughing in the sun; whoever came up and saw the sight, soon asked for a glass to try a sample; then he would stand there with his eyes watering as he felt its sweetness and comfort coursing through him. And the sweet apple juice filled the air around with its cheerful, strong delicious smell. It is the best smell of the whole year, the very essence of ripeness and harvest, and it is good to get it into one's nostrils before the oncoming winter for then you remember with gratitude a host of good and wonderful things: gentle May rain, rippling sunshine, cool autumn-morning dew, tender spring sunlight, shining summer heat, glowing white and rose-red blossom, the ripe red brown gleam of the fruit trees before the fruit is gathered and among it all the beauty and pleasure the year's cycle has brought with it.

These were good days for everybody. The wealthy and superior folk, in so far as they condescended to appear in person, weighed their large apples in their hands, counted their dozen or more sacks, drank samples of cider from a silver beaker and let it be known that there was no drop of water in their cider. The poor people could only provide a single sack of fruit. They sampled the juice in glasses or earthenware dishes and added water, but they were not a whit less proud or cheerful about it. Those who, for any reason, were unable to produce any cider themselves, went along to neighbours or acquaintances, from one press to another, were given a glass of it to drink, pocketed an apple and showed by their connoisseur remarks that they too understood their part in this business. The many children, however, rich and poor alike, ran about with little mugs; all of them carried an apple they had bitten into in one hand and a hunk of bread in the other, for as long as anyone could remember there had been a saying—quite groundless—that if you ate bread at the cider harvest you did not get the colic.

Hundreds of voices called out at the same time quite

apart from the row the children were making. All the voices were excited and cheerful.

" Come over 'ere Hannes ! Just a glass ! "

" Ee, thanks but oi've gotten the colic already ! "

" 'Ow much did ee pay a 'undredweight ? "

" Four bob. But they be foin. Just try un."

Sometimes a slight mishap occurred. A sack of apples fell open before it was intended and they all rolled out on the ground.

" 'Oly Moses, my apples ! Help, all on you ! "

They all helped to pick them up and only a few ragamuffins tried to enrich themselves.

" Eh you varmint, don't pocket any ! Eat as many as ee loikes but don't ee tuck 'em away. Just you wait, you half-baked little sod."

" Eh, neighbour, don't ee be so proud ! Just sample `un. They be sweet as honey ! How much 'av ee made then ? "

" Two barrel, not more. But all good stuff."

" Good thing we don't make cider at midsummer, else us 'ud drink it all straightaway."

There were a few peevish old folk present who would not miss the celebration. They had not made cider now for some time but they knew more about it and talked about the year dot when the fruit was almost given away. Everything was so much cheaper and better and there was no question of adding sugar in those days, the trees bore such good fruit.

" They could talk about zider 'arvest in them days. I 'ad an apple-tree that produced foive 'undred-weight just by hissen." Bad though times had now become, these old grumblers did not mind lending a hand now, and those who still possessed any teeth chewed away at their apple. One of them had done his best with some large pears and was suffering from colic.

" That's what oi was sayin'," he grumbled, " in olden toimes oi've eaten ten of 'em straight off." And he fetched three great sighs as he thought of the time when he could eat ten of these large pears before he got belly-ache.

Herr Flaig had his cider-press in the middle of the crowd and enlisted the help of the older apprentice. He got his apples from the Baden district and his cider was always the best. He was quietly contented and made no attempt to discourage anyone from trying a sample. His children who moved round him quite cheerfully among the throng were even more contented. But most contented of all, though he did not show it, was his apprentice. He felt pleased in every bone in his body to be able to go about busily in the open air, for he had his origins in a poor peasant's hut in the forest and he revelled in the delicious feeling of well-being that he got from the wonderful sweetness. His healthy peasant boy's face wore a grin like a satyr's and his cobbler's hands were washed cleaner even than on Sundays.

When Hans Giebenrath arrived at the square he was quiet and nervous; he had not been keen to attend. But a beaker was held out to him at the first press he came to, by Naschold's Liese in point of fact. He tried it and as he swallowed it a flood of gay memories of previous autumns accompanied the sweet, heady cider taste and a tentative longing to join in the merriment again. Acquaintances addressed him, glasses were offered, and by the time he came to Flaig's press, the general cheerfulness and the drink had completely transformed him. He greeted the cobbler dutifully and made a few of the traditional quips about the cider. Hiding his astonishment Flaig bade him welcome.

Half an hour had passed when a girl in a blue skirt arrived, smiled at the cobbler and his apprentice and began to help them.

" Yes," said the shoemaker, " this is my niece from Heilbronn. She's used to a different kind of autumn; hers is a wine-growing district."

She might have been eighteen or nineteen years old, animated and cheerful as lowlanders are; she was on the small side but had a generous figure and held herself well. Her dark, warm eyes and the pretty, kissable mouth were gay and intelligent in her round face. She looked the truly healthy and vivacious native of Heilbronn that she was, though hardly a relation of the pious cobbler. She belonged completely to this world and her eyes were not those of a person accustomed to reading the Bible at night and Gossner's " Treasury."

Hans suddenly looked distressed and wished with all his being that Emma would go away. But she stayed there, laughing and chattering, with a ready answer for every jest, and Hans grew embarrassed and fell silent. He hated going round with girls with whom he had to be on grown-up terms and this one was so lively and talkative and so indifferent to his presence and awkwardness that he drew in his horns helplessly and, slightly offended, withdrew into himself like a snail brushed by a cart-wheel. He stood still and tried to assume an expression of indifference, but he was unsuccessful; he looked instead like someone who has just suffered a bereavement.

Nobody had time to pay any heed to him, Emma least of all. She had been staying for the last fortnight with Flaig.

Hans heard, but she already knew everybody in the town. She mixed with high and low alike, sampled the new cider, laughed and joked, came back again and behaved as if she was part of it all, took the children in her arms, gave apples away and spread laughter and gaiety round her. " Do you want an apple ? " she shouted to every street boy. And she would take a handsome, rosy-cheeked apple, stretch her hands behind her back and let them guess. " Which hand is it in, left or right ? " But the apple was never where they thought and only when the boys began grumbling did she hand it over, and then it would turn out to be a smaller, green apple. She seemed to know all about Hans, asked him whether he was the boy who was always having headaches and before he had time to reply had already embarked on another conversation with people round her. Hans was of a mind to sneak off home when Flaig put the press lever in his hand.

" Well, you can do a bit more work now; Emma will help you. I must go back to the shop."

Flaig went off, the apprentice was instructed to help his mistress to cart the cider away and Hans was left alone at the press with Emma. He gritted his teeth and worked like a fiend.

Then he began to wonder why the lever was so heavy to turn and when he looked up, Emma burst out into a peal of bell-like laughter. She had leant firmly against it and when Hans pulled at it again, furious, she repeated her tactics.

He did not say a word but as he worked the lever which the girl resisted with her body at the other side, he suddenly felt embarrassed and awkward and gradually stopped turning. A kind of delicious panic swept over him and when the girl laughed cheekily in his face, she

148

suddenly looked quite different, at the same time more friendly and more of a stranger. Now he too laughed a little, confidently but not quite at his ease.

Then the lever stopped working altogether.

And Emma said, " We won't go so hard at it," and handed him a half-filled glass out of which she herself had been drinking.

This draught of cider seemed very strong, sweeter than the one before and when he had drunk it, he gazed wistfully into the empty glass and was surprised to find how fast his heart was beating and how hard his breath came.

After that they worked a short time again and Hans hardly knew what he was doing when he found himself contriving to stand in a position where the girl's skirt would brush against him and her hand touch his. Every time it happened his heart stopped in panic-stricken bliss and a feeling of exquisite weakness swept over him and his knees trembled a little and there was a dizzy, rushing sound in his head.

He did not know what he was saying but he had a ready reply for everything, laughed when she laughed, wagged his finger at her a few times when she played the fool, and drank up the two glasses of cider she handed him. At the same time a whole host of memories raced through his mind. Housemaids he had seen standing with men in doorways at night, odd snatches from story books, the kiss which Hermann Heilner had given him and lots of sayings, tales and surreptitious conversations heard at school about " wenches " and what it was like to have a sweetheart. And he breathed great sighs like an old nag struggling up a mountain side. Everything was transformed. The people and the activity round about him dissolved into a coloured and glorious cloud of well-being. The isolated voices, curses and laughter were submerged in a general melancholy and the river and the old bridge looked far away like pieces of painted scenery.

Even Emma looked different. He no longer saw her face, all he saw were her dark, cheerful eyes and scarlet lips and her white pointed teeth behind them; her form seemed to melt away—and he only saw an isolated part—now a shoe and an area of black stocking, now a stray curl on her neck, now her rounded, sunburnt throat plunging into the blue scarf, now the braced shoulders and her heaving breast below, now a translucent pink ear.

And after a while she let the beaker fall into the vat and bent over it and in so doing pressed her knee against the side of the vat and against his wrist. And he stooped down too but more slowly and almost brushed his face against her hair. Her hair had a faint scent and in the middle of it, behind the shadow of some loose curls glowed a warm, brown neck which disappeared into the blue bodice whose tight lacing in the lower part allowed the eye to follow it a further distance down the opening.

When she straightened herself up and in the process her knee had touched his arm and her hair brushed his cheek and her cheeks were quite flushed with stooping, a great shudder ran through Hans' limbs. He turned pale and for a moment was conscious of a deep-seated weakness inside him and he had to cling to the press lever for support. His heart was beating furiously, his arms became limp and he felt a pain in his shoulders.

From this point on he scarcely uttered another word and avoided her glance. But he riveted his eyes on her as soon as she turned away, with mixed feelings of guilt and newly found excitement. At that moment something inside him seemed to break and a new, strangely alluring land with distant blue shores opened up before his soul. He did not yet know, or had only a vague idea what this panic and exquisite torment within him signified nor could he have said which was greater, pain or joy.

But the joy meant the victory of his youthful sensuality and the first stirrings of the full vigour of life; the pain meant that the peace of the morning of his life was broken and that his soul had left the land of childhood which one never re-discovers. His light bark, after a first narrow escape from shipwreck, had now encountered the full force of fresh storms and approached shallows and dizzy cliffs between which youth, for all its previous guidance, must find its own way to safety and salvation.

Luckily the apprentice arrived back by this time and could relieve him at the press. Hans stayed there a while longer, hoping for a caress or a friendly word from Emma. She was chatting once more alongside other cider-presses. Feeling awkward in front of the apprentice, he soon hurried home without saying goodbye.

Everything had become strangely different, wonderful, exciting. The sparrows fattened on the apple pulp and flew off noisily into the sky which had never before seemed so high and beautiful and idyllically blue. Never before had the river had such a limpid, blue-green, smiling surface, nor had the weir ever been such a roar of dazzling white. It all stood before him like a series of decorative paintings behind fresh, clear glass.

Everything seemed to be waiting for the start of a great feast. Even in his own breast he felt a constricting, frightening yet wonderful surge of strangely bold emotions and lively and unwonted hopes, mixed with a doubting fear that it was all a dream and could never come true. These conflicting emotions swelled into a darkly moving tide, a feeling that something overwhelmingly strong must burst inside him and find its way into the open, in a fit of weeping perhaps, or a song, or a peal of laughter. Only when he reached home did this excitement abate a little. At home everything was just the same as ever.

"Where have you come from ? " asked Herr Giebenrath.

" Flaig's by the mill."

" How much cider has he produced ? "

" Two barrels, I think."

He asked to be allowed to invite the Flaig children in if old Flaig came to the cider feast.

" Naturally," muttered his father. " I'm making it next week. Bring them along."

There was still an hour to go before supper time. Hans went out into the garden. Apart from the two fir trees there was not much green to be seen. He tore off a hazel twig, swished it through the air and stirred about with it in the withered foliage. The sun was already behind the mountain whose black outline was silhouetted against the blue-green, misty late evening sky, showing the hair-lines of the pine-tree tops. A grey elongated cloud, suffused with golden brown sailed at a comfortable leisurely pace through the thin gold air up the valley, like a homecoming ship.

Hans strolled through the garden in an odd manner for him, before the opulent, colourful beauty of sunset. He paused at intervals, closed his eyes and tried to picture Emma as she had stood opposite him by the cider press. He went over in his mind how she had got him to drink from her cup, how she had bent over the vat and the flush on her face when she had straightened her back. He saw her hair, her figure in the tight blue bodice, her breast and the nape of her neck, shadowed with dark hairs. Delicious shivers ran through him, but try as he might, he was no longer able to recall her face.

When the sun had set, he did not notice the chill of the air; the invading twilight seemed like a veil full of secrets which he could not name. For he realized that he had fallen in love with the Heilbronn girl but he recognized these stirrings of awakening manhood only vaguely as part of an unwonted, over-excited and exhausting condition.

It felt strange at supper to be sitting in his transformed state of mind among the old familiar surroundings. His father, the old maid-servant, table and utensils suddenly looked old and he saw everything with a feeling of surprise, strangeness and affection, as if he had just returned home from a long journey. In those days when his eyes had dwelt affectionately on his chosen branch, he had regarded these same beings and objects with the melancholy and pondered emotion of one ready to take his leave, but now it was a home-coming, a surprise, a smile, a rehabilitation.

They had had supper and Hans was about to get up when his father remarked in his brusque way " How would you like to be a mechanic, Hans; or would you rather become a clerk ? "

" But how ? " asked Hans astounded.

" You could be apprenticed to Herr Schuler, the mechanic, at the end of the week or start the week after next as a pupil in the Townhall. Think it over ! We'll discuss it further to-morrow."

Hans stood up and left the room. He was dazed and confused by the suddenness of the question. The busy, fresh everyday life to which he had been a stranger for months stood unexpectedly before him, presenting an attractive yet threatening face, full of promises and demands. He had no desire to be either a mechanic or a clerk. He found

153

the prospect of strenuous physical work somewhat frightening. Then he remembered his school friend August, who had already become a mechanic and whom he could question about it.

As he turned the matter over, his ideas on the subject became more gloomy and uncertain; the affair seemed less urgent and important. He had something very different on his mind. Restless, he paced up and down the hall, suddenly picked up his hat, left the house and walked slowly up the street. He had suddenly felt that he must see Emma again that day.

It was already growing dark. Cries and raucous singing rang out from a neighbouring inn. Lights showed in a number of windows; here and there first one lit up and then another, giving a pale red glow in the darkness. A long line of girls, arm in arm, came strolling down the street, laughing and chattering, wavered in the uncertain light, then surged through the sleepy streets like a warm wave of youth and happiness. Hans gazed after them for a little time; he felt a throbbing in his arteries. Someone could be heard playing the violin behind a curtained window. A woman was washing lettuces at the pump. Two young men were strolling over the bridge with their sweethearts. One of them, who was holding his girl loosely by the arm, let go of it and smoked his cigar. The second couple walked along slowly, closely linked, the man encircled the girl's waist with his arm and she leaned her head and shoulders against his breast. Hans had seen this kind of thing hundreds of times without giving it any thought but now it took on a secret meaning, a vague, sensual but charming significance. His eyes rested on the group and his imagination strained to understand it all. Uneasy, profoundly shaken within, he felt close to a great secret, not knowing whether it was wonderful or dreadful but merely apprehensive before either possibility.

He stopped before Flaig's cottage but was unable to pluck up sufficient courage to enter. What was he to say or do once he was inside ? He could not help remembering the many times when he had come here as a boy of eleven or twelve years old. In those days Flaig had told him Bible stories and satisfied his impetuous curiosity about hell, the devil and evil spirits. They were uncomfortable memories and gave him a feeling of guilt. He did not know what he should do; he did not even know what he wanted, yet it seemed to him that he was face to face with something secret and forbidden. He felt that he was acting unfairly towards the shoemaker in standing thus in the darkness before his door without entering. And if the latter saw him standing there or stepping down from the doorway, he would probably not even tell him off; he would just laugh. It was that he dreaded most of all.

He slipped round the house and could now see from the garden fence into the lighted living-room. He could not see Flaig himself. His wife appeared to be sewing or knitting; the eldest boy was still up and sat at the table, reading. Emma was moving round, evidently busy clearing up so that he could only catch momentary glimpses of her. It was so quiet that it was possible to hear clearly every distant step in the street and, from the other side of the garden, the gentle murmur of the river. Darkness and the chill of night were rapidly descending.

A smaller hall window was situated close to those of the living-room. After a while an indistinguishable form appeared at the first, leaned out and peered into the night. Hans recognized the figure as that of Emma and full of apprehensive hope, his heart stood still. She gazed long and calmly from the window but Hans did not know whether she would see and recognize him. He did not move as he looked towards her, hoping and at the same time in some trepidation lest she might recognize him.

And the vague form disappeared from the window; immediately afterwards followed the click of the little garden gate, and Emma emerged from the house. In his first panic Hans felt an impulse to run away but he stayed leaning against the fence powerless to move and saw the girl walking slowly towards him down the dark garden and at every step she took, he felt the same desire to run away, but he was held back by something stronger than himself.

Now Emma stood exactly in front of him, not half a yard away, with only the low fence between them, and looked at him with an odd searching gaze. For a while she did not speak, then she said softly, " What do you want ? "

" Nothing," he said, and her affectionate tone was like a caress.

She stretched her hand out to him over the fence. He took it shyly and tenderly and gave it a gentle squeeze; then, noticing that she did not withdraw it, plucked up courage and delicately stroked her warm hand. When she let him continue to hold it, he laid it against his cheek. A flood of desire, unwonted warmth and agreeable lassitude went through him and he seemed conscious of a damp, warm breeze stirring about him and the street and garden melted away and all he saw was a bright face close beside him and a riot of dark hair.

And her voice appeared to reach him from far-off in the night when she said gently, " Won't you kiss me ? "

Her glowing face came closer, the pressure of her body bent the fence back slightly; her loose, faintly scented hair brushed against Hans' forehead, and closed eyes with broad white lids and dark lashes confronted his. A shudder ran through him as he touched the girl's mouth with his own shy lips. He shrank back a moment trembling but she took his head between her hands, pressed her face to his and would not leave his lips. He felt her mouth burning as she pressed it against his as if she wanted to drain the life out of them. He was overcome with a great weakness but before her lips let him go, his trembling desire had changed into a deathly weariness and pain and when Emma released him, he tottered and clung hard to the fence with convulsive fingers.

" Be back here again to-morrow, darling," Emma said and ran back swiftly into the house. But to Hans it seemed an eternity. His eyes followed her blankly, he still clung to the fence boarding too exhausted to take a step away. Half in a dream he could hear the blood as it pounded at his temples and raced to his heart and back in irregular, painful surges, making him gasp for breath.

Now he saw the doors in the room open and in walked Flaig who had certainly just left his workshop. A fear that he might be seen came over Hans and drove him away. He walked slowly, reluctantly and unsteadily as if he was slightly drunk and at every step he made he had the feeling that his knees might give way. The dark streets with their sleepy gables and sad, red window peep-holes flowed past him like faded pieces of stage scenery, then bridges, river, courtyards and gardens. The Gerberstrasse fountain splashed strangely loud and echoing. Half asleep he opened and shut first one door and then another, sat down on a table that stood there and only after some time did he awake to the discovery that he was in the living-room at home. It was some time before he could bring himself to get undressed. He did so in an absent-minded fashion and sat undressed by the window until the autumn night air sent a cold shudder through him and drove him on to the pillows.

He thought he was bound to fall asleep at any moment but he had no sooner lain down than his heart began to thump and he was conscious of the blood throbbing in his arteries. When he closed his eyes, he felt as if Emma's lips were still hanging from his, drawing out his soul and filling him with a fever-heat.

Late during the night he fell asleep and rushed headlong from one dream to the next in a frantic chase. He stood in the midst of a darkness that was terrifyingly profound, and groping about, he seized hold of Emma's arm; she embraced him and they sank down together slowly in a deep warm tide. The shoemaker suddenly stood before him and asked why he would not call on him and Hans could not help laughing and then he noticed that it was not Flaig at all but Hermann Heilner who was sitting next to him in a window embrasure in the Maulbronn oratory, making jokes. But that too soon faded and he was standing by the cider press, Emma was leaning against the lever and he was pushing against her weight with all his might. She was stooping over it, feeling for his lips and it grew still and dark and now he was sinking back into the warm, dark depths fainting with giddiness. Simultaneously he could hear the Principal making a speech but he could not make out whether or not it was directed at him.

He slept on far into the morning. It was a bright, sunny day. He walked slowly to and fro in the garden, endeavouring to shake off his sleepiness and clear his head but he was unable to shake off the heavy mist of sleep. He could see violet asters, the very last flowers standing in the garden, beautiful and gay in the sunshine as if it were still August, and he saw the warm, attractive light round the withered branches and twigs, and leafless vine shoots trailing invitingly around as if it was the period just before Spring. But it was only with his eyes that he saw it all, not his mind, so that it had no effect on his mood. Suddenly he was in the grip of a clear, vivid memory of the time when his tame hares had leapt about here in the garden and his waterwheel and hammermill still worked. His memory jerked him back to a September morning three years ago. It was the evening before the Sedan anniversary. His friend August had come to him bringing a bunch of ivy and then they had washed down their flag-poles until they were shining and fastened the ivy to the golden spikes, as they chatted about the next day and looked forward to it. Nothing else had happened, but they had been both so filled with joyful anticipation of the festivity, the banners had shone in the sun, Anna had baked plum cakes and at night the Sedan bonfire was to be lit on the high mountain ridge.

Hans did not know why to-day in particular, his mind should go back to that evening, why the recollection of it was so vivid and attractive nor why it made him so sad and wretched. He did not realize that his childhood and adolescence stood before him happy and smiling, clothed in this memory ready to say farewell and leave behind the sting of a great happiness that had once been and was never to return. He just felt vaguely that this memory did not fit in with his thoughts of Emma and the evening before, and that something had arisen in him that could not be linked up with his previously experienced happiness. He believed

159

he could see the golden spikes of the banner-poles shining, hear his friend August laugh and smell the fragrance of the freshly-baked cakes, and it was all so gay and happy and had become so strange and remote that he leant back against the trunk of the huge red pine and broke into a helpless fit of sobbing which afforded him momentary relief and comfort.

At mid-day he hurried over to August who had now become senior apprentice and had left him far behind in physical growth and experience. Hans unburdened himself.

"That's just it," commented August, "That's just it. Just because you're so weak in maths. They always give you the hammering to do the first year and the hammer is no soup-ladle. You have to lug the tools around and clear up in the evening, and filing's quite an art, and to begin with until you get the hang of it you pick up hopeless old files which won't work and are as smooth as a baby's bottom."

Hans was depressed.

"Well, I had better leave it alone, hadn't I?" he asked hesitatingly.

"Rot! Don't say that! Don't be a softy! It's just that it's not all beer and skittles to start with. But then there's something grand about being a mechanic and you've got to have a good head or else you'll end up as a blacksmith. Take a look at this!"

He produced a few small, finely worked machine parts in shining steel and showed them to Hans.

"They mustn't be a half-millimetre out. All done by hand right down to the screws. You've got to have sharp eyes for that. They have to be polished and tempered, then they're ready.

"Yes, that's wonderful. If I only knew . . . "

August laughed.

"Are you nervous? Yes, a beginner gets told off and that doesn't help. But I'll be there to lend you a hand. And if you make a start next Friday, I shall have completed my second year by then and will be getting my first weekly wage on Saturday. And I'll be celebrating on Sunday with beer and cakes and all the lads will be there and you'll see what a lark we have. Ah, now you're looking interested! After all we were good pals in the old days."

During dinner Hans told his father that he wanted to be a mechanic and asked whether he could begin in a week's time.

"Right you are," said his father and accompanied him to the Schuler's workshop in the afternoon and signed him up.

By time it was dusk, however, Hans had almost forgotten all about it; all he remembered was that Emma would be expecting him that evening. He could hardly breathe, time seemed alternately to race by and then drag and he approached the rendezvous like a boatman preparing to shoot the rapids. He could not possibly eat his supper that night. He managed however to swallow down a glass of milk. Then he started out.

It was just like the day before—dark, drowsy streets, glowing windows, hazy lamp-light, strolling couples.

On reaching the cobbler's garden fence he was overcome by a great panic; he shuddered at every sound and felt like a thief lurking around in the darkness. He had hardly been there a minute when Emma stood before him, ran her hands through his hair and opened the garden gate. He entered cautiously and she drew him gently along the shrub-bordered path, through the back door and into the dark passage inside.

There they sat side by side on the top cellar step and it was some time before their eyes had become sufficiently accustomed to the darkness to see anything of each other. Emma was in a good mood and chattered away in a whisper. She had tasted many a kiss in the past and knew all about love-making; this shy, affectionate boy suited her. She took his narrow face between her hands and kissed his forehead, eyes and cheeks and when it came to the turn of his lips she kissed him with the same lingering kiss as on the previous occasion. Hans was overcome with giddiness and leaned against her limp and irresolute. She gave a soft laugh and pinched his ear.

Then she chattered away again and he listened but without any idea of what she was talking about. She stroked his arm, hair, neck and hand, pressed her cheek against his and leaned her head on his shoulders. He kept silent and remained passive, filled with a kind of delicious horror and a profound, joyful panic, giving an occasional short, gentle shudder like a man smitten with fever.

" What a lover you are ! " she laughed. " You seem frightened of yourself."

And she took his hand and passed it over her neck, through her hair and laid it against her breast and pressed it there. He could feel its soft shape and the strange, wonderful heaving, closed his eyes and seemed to fall away into bottomless depths. " No, no more ! " he said, fending her off when she tried to kiss him again. She laughed.

She drew him close to her pressing his side against hers, twining her arm round him so that feeling her body against him, his reason fled and he was utterly bereft of speech.

" Do you love me then ? " she asked.

162

He tried to say " yes " but all he could do was to nod and he kept on nodding for some time.

She took his hand again and pushed it with a laugh under her bodice. His heart stopped as he felt the throb of her arteries and her warm breath so close to him and he thought he would suffocate, so difficult did he find it to breathe. He withdrew his hand, moaned " I must go home now."

When he tried to stand up, he began to totter and nearly fell head over heels down the cellar stairs.

" What's the matter ? " asked Emma, astounded.

" I don't know. I am so tired."

He did not notice that she supported him on their way back to the garden gate and pressed herself against him nor hear her say goodnight and close the little gate behind him. He did not know how he found his way through the streets—it was as if a great storm tore him along or a tidal wave was tossing him to and fro.

He saw the pale glow from the houses on the right and left, mountain ridges and pine-tree tops on the slopes above and over them all the blackness of night and the peaceful stars. He felt the wind blow, heard the river murmur as it flowed past the bridge piles and saw the gardens, shadowy houses, the dark night, street lights and stars mirrored in the water.

He was forced to sit down on the bridge; he was so tired, and he thought he would never get home. As he sat on the parapet he listened to the water sliding by the piers, roaring over the weir and gurgling by the mill-dam. His hands were cold, his blood flowed jerkily in his chest and throat, brought a mist before his eyes and raced back to his heart and head in a sudden gush until he became giddy.

He arrived home, found his way to his own room, lay down and at once fell asleep, sinking in his dreams from one depth to another in infinite space. He woke up, exhausted and in torment and lay between sleeping and waking until the morning, filled with an unquenchable longing and tossed hither and thither by uncontrollable forces until in the early dawn his torment and oppression found release in a prolonged fit of weeping and he fell asleep again on tear-stained pillows.

CHAPTER SEVEN

Herr Giebenrath worked away at the cider press with dignity and a good deal of noise and Hans helped him. Two of the cobbler's children had accepted his invitation and busied themselves with the fruit, sampled a glass of the juice and clutched huge hunks of black-bread in their fists. But Emma had not accompanied them.

Only when his father had gone away half an hour with the cooper did Hans venture to ask about her.

" Where's Emma ? Couldn't she come ? "

It was a little time before the young children's mouths were empty enough to reply.

" She's gone away," they said and nodded.

"Away, where ? "

" Home."

" Gone off by train ? "

The children nodded vigorously.

" When ? "

" This morning."

The children reached out for their apples. Hans walked round with the press lever, stared into the cider vat and the truth slowly dawned on him.

His father returned; they worked away laughing and joking; the children said goodbye and ran off; evening descended and they all went home.

After supper Hans sat in his room alone. It struck ten, then eleven but he did not light the lamp. Then he fell into a long deep sleep.

When he finally awoke it was later than usual and he

was conscious only of a vague feeling of loss and calamity until he remembered about Emma. She had left without even saying goodbye; yet she must have known when she intended to leave the place during the last evening he had spent at her house. He thought of her laugh and kisses and her deliberate surrender at that time. She had not taken him seriously. The restlessness caused by his excited and unsatisfied passion and his bitter sorrow became part of the sad torment which drove him away from the house into the garden, the street, the woods and back home again.

Such was his first, perhaps too early, experience of love's secrets and it held a good deal more bitterness than sweetness. Days of fruitless complaint, poignant memories, desperate heart-searchings; nights when his pounding heart and a feeling of tightness within him prevented him from sleeping or plunged him into terrible nightmares. Nightmares in which the mysterious stir of his blood was transformed into monstrous and terrifying fairy-tale illustrations, deathly, embracing arms, hot-eyed, horrible monsters, dizzy precipices, giant, flaming eyes. He would wake up and find himself alone, surrounded by the loneliness of the cool autumn night; he longed for his sweetheart and moaning he buried his head in the tear-stained pillows.

The Friday when he was to start his apprenticeship at the mechanic's shop drew nearer. His father bought him a set of blue overalls and a blue half-woollen cap; he tried the outfit on. He thought he looked silly in this locksmith's uniform and felt miserable as he walked past the school building, the headmaster's house or that of the mathematics master, Flaig's workshop or the vicarage. So much torment, hard work and sweat, so many little pleasures given up, so much pride and ambition and hopeful dreaming sacrificed, all in vain in order that now, later than the rest of his school friends and jeered at by them all, he could enter a workshop as an apprentice !

What would Heilner say about it ?

It was some time before he could reconcile himself to the locksmith's blue overalls and look forward to the Friday when he was to be initiated. At any rate it was a new experience !

But such reflexions were not much more than rare flashes among dark clouds. He could not forget Emma's departure nor did his body forget, or in any way become indifferent to, the exhilaration of those days. It longed desperately for more, clamoured for the release of its awakened desire. And so time crept slowly by in this oppressive and agonising way.

Autumn was more beautiful than ever, full of soft sunlight, with silvery mornings, bright, smiling mid-days, clear evenings. The more distant mountains assumed a deep velvety blue, the chestnut trees shone golden yellow and the wild vine hung purple over walls and fences.

Hans was ill at ease with himself in this flight from reality. In the day-time he strolled round the town and fields, avoided people, thinking they were bound to notice his torment. In the evening, however, he went into the street, looked at every maid-servant and crept guiltily in the wake of every pair of lovers. With Emma everything seemed worth striving for and all the magic of life had seemed close at hand; now it had spitefully vanished away. He forgot all the torture and uneasiness he had felt in her presence. If only he could have her back again he would no longer be shy; he would extort from her all her secrets and penetrate right into the enchanted garden of love whose door had just been shut in his face. The whole of his imagination had become entangled in the stifling, dangerous thicket, was wandering despondently in the midst of it all and, in its obstinate self-torment, refused to acknowledge that beautiful, wide, airy and friendly spaces were to be found outside the narrow magic circle.

In the end he was glad when Friday, previously awaited with apprehension, came round. Early in the morning he donned his blue overalls, put on his cap and descended the Gerbersrasse somewhat nervously in the direction of the Schuler's workshop. A few acquaintances looked at him inquisitively and one of them asked, "What's happening; have you become a locksmith?"

They were already hard at work in the smithy; the master smith had a piece of red-hot iron on the anvil at that precise moment. An assistant was wielding the heavy sledge hammer, the master applying the finer, shaping blows, holding the iron in the tongs and striking rhythmically on the anvil with his hand hammer so that it rang through the wide-open door, clear and bright into the morning.

At the long bench, blackened with oil and iron filings stood the older assistant and next to him August; each of them busy at his vice. From the ceiling above came the purr of rapidly moving belts which drove the lathes, grindstone, bellows and drilling machine, for everything was worked by water-power. August nodded to his friend as he entered, indicating that he was to wait by the door until the master had time to attend to him.

Hans stole a shy glance at the forge, lathes, the whirring belts and pulley-wheels. When the master had finished the job he came over and extended a large, warm hand. "Hang your cap up there," he said, pointing to a vacant nail on the wall.

"Come along. That's your place and your vice."

With that he led him in front of the rearmost vice and first demonstrated how he should manage his vice and keep his bench and tools in good order.

" Your father has already told me you're no Hercules and it's pretty obvious. To start with you can keep away from the forge, that is until you're a bit tougher."

He groped under the bench and extracted an iron cogwheel.

" You can start on that. The cogwheel is still rough from the furnace and is covered with little knobs and ridges. They've got to be filed off, otherwise it damages the fine machinery."

He clamped the wheel in the vice, picked up an old file and showed him how it should be done.

" Well now, you go on with it. But don't use any other of my files ! It'll keep you busy until mid-day. Then you can show me it. You don't have to worry about anything except your instructions. An apprentice doesn't need to think."

Hans began filing.

" Stop ! " shouted the master. " Not like that. Place your left hand on the file. Or are you left handed ? "

" No."

" Well then; that will be all right ! "

He went off to his own vice, the one by the door and Hans watched how he set about it.

As he made his first strokes he was surprised that the wheel was so soft and wore down so easily. Then he saw that it was only the brittle top skin that peeled off and that the granular corn that he had to file down was underneath. He made an effort and went hard at it. He had never since the days of childish toys had the pleasure of seeing something visible and useful emerge from his hands.

169

"Not so fast," shouted the master. "You must keep time when you file; one-two, one two and press on it; otherwise you'll spoil the file."

Now the senior assistant had something to do at the lathe and Hans was unable to resist the temptation to have a look. A steel drill was fitted into the chuck, the belt moved over and the shining drill buzzed round while the assistant removed the fine, glinting steel shavings.

Everywhere around were tools, lumps of iron, steel and brass, half-finished jobs, shining wheels, chisels, drills, turner's chisels and awls of every shape and size. Next to the forge hung hammers, top and bottom tools, tongs, soldering irons; along the walls were rows of files, cutting-files; on the ledges lay oil rags, small brushes, emery-paper, saws and oil-cans, bottles, boxes of nails and screws. The grindstone was almost perpetually in use.

Hans noted with satisfaction that his hands had already become quite black and he hoped his overalls would soon look a little more used for they still looked horribly new and blue compared with the grimy, patched overalls of the others.

As the morning strode by, life from the outside world continually entered. Workers arrived from the neighbouring machine knitters to have small machine parts sharpened or repaired. A farmer came and made inquiries about a mangle of his they were repairing and cursed heartily when he heard that it was not ready. Then a smartly dressed factory owner appeared and the master took him off into a side room.

In the midst of all this the work of the shop on the part of men, wheels and driving belts alike, went smoothly on, and for the first time in his life Hans heard and understood the poetry of labour which had, for the beginner at any rate, something gripping and agreeably exciting about it, and he saw his own small person and insignificant life caught up in one great rhythm.

There was a quarter of an hour break at nine o'clock and everybody received a hunk of bread and a glass of cider. August now took an opportunity of greeting the new apprentice. He spoke a few encouraging words and then began to rave about the following Sunday when he and his friends would be going off to celebrate his first wages. Hans asked him what sort of a wheel they had given him to file and learned that it belonged to a turret clock. August wanted to show Hans the part it would play in the mechanism later but at that point the senior assistant began to file again and they all quickly returned to their places.

When it was between ten and eleven o'clock, Hans began to feel tired; his knees and his right arm ached slightly. He tried putting his weight first on one leg and then the other and surreptitiously stretched them but it did not help. Then he put the file down for a moment and leaned against the vice. No one paid any attention to him. As he stood there resting and heard the belts whirring above him, he felt slightly dizzy and he had to close his eyes for a minute. Suddenly he found the master standing behind him.

" Now then, what's the trouble ? Tired already ? "

" Yes, a bit," Hans confessed.

The assistants laughed.

" It'll be all right soon," said the master calmly. " You can come along now and see how soldering is done ! "

Hans watched the soldering operation fascinated. First the soldering iron was heated, then the heated part was dusted over with chlorate of zinc and then the white metal dropped from the hot iron and hissed gently.

" Take a rag and clean the thing well. Zinc chlorate corrodes so you've not got to leave any on the metal surface."

After that Hans stood in front of his vice again and scratched around on the little wheel with his file. His arm ached and his left hand which he had to press on the file had become sore and began to smart.

At mid-day when the chief assistant put his file away and went to the wash-basin, Hans took his work to the master. The latter gave it a quick glance.

" It's all right; you can leave it at that. There's another wheel like it in the box under your bench. You start on that this afternoon."

Now Hans washed his hands too and went off. He had an hour for lunch.

Two errand boys, former schoolfellows, followed him down the street, jeering at him.

" Landexamen locksmith ! " called out one.

He quickened his pace. He did not know really whether he was content or not; he had enjoyed it in the workshop but he felt so tired, so desperately tired.

And in the porch even while he was anticipating the pleasure of sitting down and having something to eat, he suddenly remembered Emma. He had forgotten about her all the morning. He quietly adjourned to his little room, threw himself on the bed and groaned with misery. He wanted to weep but his eyes were dried up. He saw himself once more a victim of his consuming but hopeless passion. His head felt as if it would split in two and his throat ached with his choked-back sobs.

Dinner time was torture. He had to answer his father's questions and tell him everything; put up with all sorts of feeble witticisms for his father was in a good mood. As soon as the meal was over, Hans dashed into the garden

172

and spent a quarter of an hour dreaming in the sun, then it was time to go back to the workshop again.

Already by the end of the morning he had got his hands blistered; now they began to hurt badly and by evening they were so swollen that he could not pick anything up without pain. And before they stopped work he still had the whole shop to clear up under August's directions.

Saturday was even worse. His hands burned, his sore places had turned into blisters. The boss was in a temper and cursed at the slightest pretext. August comforted him by telling him his blisters would be healed in a few days and then his hands would have hardened and he would not feel any more soreness but Hans was desperately depressed, peered at the clock all day and scratched away hopelessly at his little wheel.

During the evening while he was clearing up August confided to him that he was going up to Bielach next day with a few friends, it would be a cheerful affair and Hans was not on any account to miss it. He would call for him at two o'clock. Hans assented although he would have preferred to spend the whole Sunday lying down at home, so tired and miserable did he feel. Old Anna gave him some ointment for his bad hands. He went to bed at eight and slept right up to the middle of the morning with the result that he had to hurry down to accompany his father to church.

During dinner he began to talk about August and explained that he wanted to go for a walk across the fields with him in the afternoon. His father raised no objection and even gave him fifty pfennig, making only one condition—that he should be back for supper.

As Hans strolled through the streets in the lovely sunshine he found himself enjoying Sunday again for the first time for months. The street looked more dignified, the sun brighter and everything in fact seemed gayer and more attractive when you had days of work with soiled hands and tired limbs behind you. He now understood the butchers and tanners, bakers and smiths who sat sunning themselves on the benches in front of their cottages and looked so royally happy, and he no longer looked down on them as pitiable members of the working class. He had an interested eye for the workmen, journeymen and apprentices as they walked along in a line or went into taverns with their hats at a slight angle and wearing white collars and well-brushed Sunday suits. For the most part artisans stuck to artisans, turners to turners, masons to masons, preserving the honour of their status, and among them locksmiths were the most superior craft and metal-workers in the foremost rank. They all had something homely about them and if they had a touch of the ingenuous and grotesque, the beauty and pride of their craft was not far below the surface—qualities that even to-day have something joyful and worthwhile to commend them and of which even the most miserable tailor's apprentice shows a pale reflection.

As the young mechanics stood calm and dignified in front of Schuler's house, nodding to passers-by and chatting among themselves, you could see that they formed a reliable community and had no need of any outside element even when pleasure-bent on Sundays.

Hans was conscious of the same feeling and was proud to be one of them. All the same he felt slightly uneasy at the prospect of the jollification planned for Sunday, knowing that when it came to the question of enjoying themselves, young mechanics did not do things by halves. They might even dance. Hans did not know how to, but thought he would be able to manage it and even embark on a mild bout of drinking if necessary. He was not used to drinking much beer and in the matter of smoking he had progressed to the stage of being able to finish a cigar without too much discomfort or disgrace.

August greeted him with festive light-heartedness. He said that the older assistant had not wanted to come but that a member of another workshop was joining them instead, so that they would at any rate be a party of four and quite enough to enliven the place. Each of them could put back as much beer as he wanted since he was paying for the lot. He offered Hans a cigar; then the four of them strolled off through the town, only quickening their pace when they had reached the Lindenplatz so that they would not be too late arriving at Bielach.

The river gleamed black, gold and white and through the almost leafless maple trees and acacias you could feel the mild October sun shining from a cloudless sky of bright blue. It was one of those quiet, clear and friendly autumn days on which all the beauty of the past summer fills the mild air like a cheerful, untroubled memory, when children forget the season and think about looking for flowers to pick, and old people with thoughtful eyes gaze into the air from the window or the bench in front of their houses as if they can see agreeable memories not only of the year but of their whole past lives flying by in the clear, blue sky. The young people however are in a cheerful mood and each one of them celebrates the beautiful day according to his propensities and temperament whether by a libation or sacrifice of some kind, song or dance or horse play, for everywhere fresh fruit cakes have been baked, new apple juice or wine lies fermenting in the cellar and fiddles and harmonicas celebrate the last fine days of the year in front of the inns and on village squares, inviting you to dance, sing or make love.

Our young friends walked rapidly ahead. Hans puffed away at his cigar with assumed indifference and was surprised to find himself feeling in good form. The journeyman talked to him about his travelling apprenticeship and none of them took exception to his boasting—it was all part of the act. Even the most modest artisan apprentice on occasion and when he is sure of an audience will tell yarns of his itinerant days in a grand and dashing style, for the wonderful poetry of the artisans' life is the common property of the people and draws out of each individual the old traditional adventures with fresh embellishments, and every wandering apprentice as he launches into a story has something in him of the immortal Till Eulenspiegel and an element of the no less immortal Straubinger.

" What a devil of a life I led in Frankfurt where I was at that time ! Did I ever tell you about the wealthy shopkeeper, an awful scoundrel incidentally, who wanted to marry my boss's daughter; but she sent him packing for she preferred me and was my sweetheart for four months and if I hadn't had a dust-up with the old man I would still be there and his son-in-law into the bargain."

And he went on to recount how his beast of a master had threatened to thrash him, the wretched slave-driver, and on one occasion had had the nerve to aim a blow at him but he had not deigned to say anything, he had merely swung his hammer and given his master such a look that the latter had walked quietly away, preferring to keep his skull intact and later chose to give him his dismissal in writing, the cowardly villain. He also told them about a big fight in Offenburg where three locksmiths, including himself, had half killed seven factory workers—whoever goes to Offenburg, he said, only need ask for big Schorsch who still lives there and was present at the time.

All this was imparted in a callous tone but yet with such verve and amiability that they all revelled in the incident and mentally decided to recount it themselves later to other comrades when the occasion offered. For every locksmith has had his master's daughter as his sweetheart and some time or other has aimed a blow with his hammer at a bad master and set about seven factory hands. Sometimes the incident takes place in Baden, sometimes in Hessen, sometimes in Switzerland; it might be a file instead of the hammer or alternatively a red-hot iron; they might be bakers or tailors instead of factory workers, but they were always the same stories and the audience always enjoyed them, for they were good ones and did honour to the trade. This does not mean that even at the present time there is any shortage of individual journeymen who have been remarkable both in experience or inventiveness—which is more or less the same thing.

August, then, was enraptured with it all. He never stopped laughing and nodded approval; he already felt halfway to being qualified and puffed tobacco smoke into the golden air with a kind of disdainful satisfaction. The narrator sustained his part, for he meant his presence to be understood as good-humoured condescension since as a fully fledged assistant he did not belong to the apprentice fraternity, particularly on a Sunday, and really should be ashamed to be helping this boy to drink away his wages.

They had followed the road a good distance downstream; now the choice was between a slowly ascending carriage way which wound uphill and a steep footpath which only

177

covered half the distance. They chose the former although it was dusty and a long way. Footpaths are for everyday use and for gentlemen taking a walk; the ordinary folk, however, that is on a Sunday, prefer a country road which has not yet lost its romantic appeal for them. Climbing up steep footpaths is for farm-workers or naturalists from the town, that is to say either for work or for a hobby, but it does not commend itself to the people. On the other hand a country road is a place you can stride along in comfort, chatting as you go, saving your shoe-leather and your best Sunday clothes, a place where you see horses and carriages, encounter or overtake other strollers, meet girls all dressed up and groups of young chaps singing as they go along, where you exchange the odd joke, stand chatting, and if you are single, chase after strings of girls or laugh at them or in the evening bring up and settle personal differences among good friends with an exchange of blows !

So they followed the carriage way as it mounted gently and amiably in a sweeping curve after the manner of people who have plenty of leisure and no wish to over-exert themselves. The journeyman removed his jacket and carried it on the end of a stick slung over his shoulder; instead of telling yarns he had now begun to whistle in a jaunty and lively fashion until an hour later they arrived at Bielach. A few gibes were directed at Hans to which he did not reply very vigorously and they were parried more eagerly by August than himself. By this time they were in front of Bielach.

The village with its tiled roofs and silver-grey thatched cottages was tucked between autumn-tinted orchards and dominated behind by dark mountain forests.

The young men could not agree as to which inn they should enter. The "Anchor" had the best beer but the "Swan" the best cakes and in the "Sharp Corner" lived the handsome innkeeper's daughter. In the end August won his point that they should patronise the "Anchor", adding with a wink that the "Sharp Corner" was not going to run away while they put down a few drinks and could still be visited later. This plan suited them all and off they went into the village past stables and squat peasant cottages with geraniums in the windows to the "Anchor" with its gold sign gleaming invitingly in the sun between two young round chestnut trees. To the chagrin of the young men who particularly wanted to be inside, the parlour was already crowded and they had to find a seat in the garden.

In the opinion of the customers the "Anchor" was a fine pub, that is to say, not one of your old country inns but a modern brick erection with too many windows, chairs instead of settles, and a clutter of tin-plate advertisements; further it boasted a town-bred waitress and a landlord who was never caught in his shirt sleeves but always wore a smart brown suit. In point of fact he was bankrupt, but he had leased his house from his chief creditor, a big brewer, and since then had become still more superior. The garden consisted of an acacia and a large wire trellis now half-overgrown with wild vine.

"Good health, you fellows!" called out the young man and clinked his glass with each of the other three. Then in order to draw attention to himself he drank off the whole glass at one draught.

"Hey there, Fräulein, you pretty thing, bring me another, there wasn't anything in that!" he shouted, and handed her his tankard across the table.

The beer was excellent, cool and not too bitter and Hans enjoyed his glass. August drank with the air of a connoisseur, clicking his tongue; at the same time he was smoking like a factory chimney and Hans was filled with quiet admiration.

It was not so bad then after all, this Sunday spree, sitting at the table as one who has earned the right to be there in the company of people who knew life and how to enjoy themselves. It was pleasant to join in their laughter and sometimes even venture a joke oneself; it was so nice and grown-up to crash your tankard on the table when you had drunk the contents and call out casually, " I'll have another, Fräulein." It was pleasant to drink to an acquaintance at another table and dangle the stub of the cigar in your left hand and push your hat on the back of your head like the other chaps.

The stranger journeyman now began to warm up and tell the tale. He knew of a locksmith in Ulm who could knock back twenty glasses of good Ulm beer and when he had finished would wipe his mouth and say, " Well, and now give me a good bottle of wine ! " And in Cannstatt he had known a fireman who could put down a dozen sausages, one after the other and had won a bet on it. But he had lost the second. He had betted he could eat every item on the menu of a small tavern and had eaten practically everything but at the end of the menu were four kinds of cheese and when he came to the third, he pushed the plate away saying, " I'd rather die than eat another bite ! "

These tales were also greeted with generous applause and demonstrated that there must be enough record-breaking eaters and drinkers in the world around to enable everybody present to produce a story about this kind of hero and his deeds. One told about a "man in Stuttgart," another about a "'dragoon' in Ludwigsburg"; in one story it had been seventeen potatoes, in another eleven pancakes with salad. These events were related with an air of solemnity and they all sat back comfortably acknowledging that there existed many marvellous gifts and remarkable men, including not a few mad eccentrics. This comfortable and practical approach is the honourable legacy of the parochial outlook to be found in every local inn and is imitated by the younger generation in the same way as they imitate their elders in matters of drinking, talking, politics, smoking, marrying and dying.

At the third glass someone asked whether there were any cakes. They summoned the waitress and received the reply that there were not, and everybody became very worked up about it. August rose and said that if there were not any cakes they could move on to another inn. Their companion from elsewhere cursed the present wretched inn; only the man from Frankfurt was for staying on. He had got on to good terms with the waitress and had already found several opportunities for fondling her. Hans had noticed this and added to the effect of the beer, it had excited him in an odd way. He was relieved that they were moving on.

When August had paid the bill and they were all in the street again Hans began to feel the effect of his three glasses. It was an agreeable sensation, a combination of weariness and a devil-may-care spirit, and he was conscious too of something like a thin mist before his eyes through which everything looked more remote, almost unreal as one sees things in a dream. He found himself laughing all the time and had put his hat on at a more rakish angle and imagined he looked the picture of a man on the razzle. The man from Frankfurt started whistling again in his aggressive way and Hans tried to walk in time to it.

It was fairly quiet at the " Sharp Corner." There were just a few farmers drinking the new season's wine. There was no draught beer to be had, only bottles, one of which was immediately set before each of the new customers. The journeyman was anxious to prove his generosity and ordered a large apple cake for them all. Hans suddenly felt terribly hungry and ate several pieces one after the other. He sat there on the broad, solid settle, dreamy and comfortable in the old brown parlour. The old-fashioned sideboard and the huge stove were lost in the semi-darkness; in a large cage furnished with wooden bars fluttered two blue-tits for which a twig with red berries had been thrust through the bars.

The landlord went up to the table for a moment and bade the guests welcome. It was a little time before a conversation was properly started. Hans drank a few gulps from the beer-bottle and wondered whether he would be able to finish it off.

Their Frankfurt acquaintance embarked once again on his fantastic tales about rhenish grape harvest feasts, his work as a journeyman and life in doss-houses, to which they listened in high spirits and Hans never stopped laughing.

Suddenly he noticed that there was something amiss with him. Room, table, bottle, glasses and the figures of his friends were all swimming dizzily together in a soft brown haze, only reassuming their detached, individual shape when he shook himself. From time to time when laughter and conversation increased in volume, he laughed aloud or made a remark which he immediately forgot.

When they clinked glasses he joined in, and an hour later, he was surprised to see that his bottle was empty.

" You've got a good thirst," said August. " Will you have another ? "

Hans nodded with a smile. He had imagined a night out as being a much more perilous affair. And now when their Frankfurt friend started a song, in which they all joined, Hans sang no less heartily than the rest.

Meantime the room had filled up and the landlord's daughter came in to lend the waitress a hand. She was a robust young Fräulein with a healthy, energetic-looking face and confident brown eyes.

When she planted a fresh bottle in front of Hans, his frivolous neighbour at once bombarded her with his flowery gallantries but she did not listen. Perhaps to show her indifference to the latter or possibly because she took a fancy to his delicate boyish head, she turned to Hans and ran her hand through his hair; then she went back to the side-board.

The journeyman, who was now drinking his third bottle, followed her and made every effort to engage her in conversation, but in vain. The robust girl glanced coldly at him without replying and then turned her back on him. He returned to the table, drummed on it with his empty glass and called out in a sudden burst of excitement, "Come on lads; enjoy yourselves; good health ! "

And he embarked on a sentimental story.

But all Hans could hear was a melancholy confusion of voices and when he had nearly finished his second bottle, he found it difficult to speak and even to laugh. He got up to walk over to the blue-tits' cage and tease the birds but after two steps he became dizzy, nearly fell down and cautiously staggered back.

From this point on his cheerful spirits gradually melted away. He knew that he was having a " blind " and the idea of the drinking bout had now lost its appeal. Lurking as it were in the distance he saw all kinds of trouble lying in wait for him: the journey home, an ugly scene with his father, and next day, the workshop. Gradually his headache came on.

The others too had had enough. August in a lucid moment asked for the bill and received very little change from his three-mark piece. They strolled down the road chattering and laughing, dazzled by the bright evening light. Hans was unable to stand upright and leaned unsteadily against August and allowed himself to be supported by him.

The journeyman had now become sentimental and was singing " To-morrow I must leave this place," with tears in his eyes.

They were about to make for home but as they passed the " Swan " the journeyman insisted on going in. Hans broke away as they came under the porch.

" I must go home."

" You'll never make it by yourself," laughed the journeyman.

" Yes, yes. I must . . . get . . . home."

" At least you must have a nip of brandy then, young 'un. It'll put you on your feet again and settle your stomach. Yes, you'll see."

Hans was conscious of a glass in his hand. He spilt a good deal of the contents and swallowed the rest down. It felt like a fire burning in his gullet. Somehow he staggered down the outside steps; he did not know how he managed to get out of the village. Houses, fences, gardens swam before his eyes in all directions.

He lay down under an apple tree in the wet meadow. Feelings of revulsion, torturing fears and fragmentary thoughts prevented him from falling asleep. He felt sullied and ashamed. How could he go home? What should he say to his father? What would happen to him to-morrow? He felt so broken and wretched as if he must rest, sleep and atone for an eternity; his head and eyes hurt him and he did not feel strong enough to stand up and continue his way.

Suddenly like a delayed, fugitive wave a hint of his former cheerfulness returned; he pulled a grimace and sang to himself:

> O du lieber Augustin,
> Augustin, Augustin,
> O du lieber Augustin,
> Alles ist hin.

But he had hardly finished singing when he felt utterly nauseated and a melancholy flood of indistinct images and memories of shame and self-reproach rose up within him. He moaned loudly and sank sobbing into the grass.

An hour later when it was already dark, he got up and staggered painfully and unsteadily downhill.

Herr Giebenrath had cursed loudly when his son failed to return for supper. When it got to be nine o'clock and Hans was still not there, he put out a stout cane which had long lain idle. The lad thought he had outgrown the paternal rod, did he? Well, he would have a nice surprise when he got home! At ten o'clock he locked the door. If his son wanted to indulge in night revels, he would soon see where he got off.

Nevertheless Herr Giebenrath did not sleep; he waited with an anger that mounted every hour to hear a hand touch the door knob and timidly pull the bell. He pictured the scene—the gadabout could learn his lesson ! Probably he would be drunk but he would soon sober him down, the blackguard, the sly boots, the miserable wretch ! If he had to break every bone in his body.

Finally sleep got the better of him and his rage.

At that same moment the object of all these threats was already slowly drifting, cold and silent down the dark waters of the river. He had shed all the revulsion, shame and sorrow; the blue chilly, autumn night looked down on his dark, slender body; the black water played over his hands and hair and bloodless lips. No one had seen him except possibly some shy otter just before dawn, eyeing him cautiously as it slid silently past. Nobody knew how he had come to be in the water. Perhaps he had strayed from the path and slipped down at some steep spot on the slope; perhaps he had been drinking and had lost his balance. Perhaps the water had exercised a fatal fascination for him as he bent over it, and night and the pale moon looked so full of peace and deep rest that weariness and fear had driven him with gentle relentlessness into the shadow of death.

They found him when it was day and took his body home. His father, horror-stricken, had to lay his rod aside and relinquish his accumulated anger. It was true that he shed no tears and displayed little emotion, but the following night he stayed awake again and now and then looked through the door-opening towards his silent child who lay on the clean bed as still as ever and who, with his refined brow and pale and intelligent face, looked like a creature apart who had an innate right to enjoy a different fate from the common run. On his brow and hands the skin was rubbed and slightly livid in hue, the handsome features were in repose, the white lids were closed over his eyes and the slightly parted lips had a contented, almost gay expression. It was as if the boy had suddenly blossomed forth and had been snatched up on his cheerful course; even his father in his weariness and solitary grief was a victim of that happy illusion.

The funeral brought a large number of followers and onlookers. Hans Giebenrath had once more become a celebrity in whom everybody was interested and once again teachers, Principal and vicar had a share in his fate. They appeared together in their frock coats and solemn top hats, followed the bier and stood by the graveside for a moment whispering among themselves. The Latin teacher looked particularly sad and the Principal murmured, " Yes, he could have become someone. Isn't is tragic that one is so often unfortunate with one's best pupils ? "

Along with his father and old Anna who wept without ceasing, Flaig stayed behind at the graveside.

" Yes, it is very hard, Herr Giebenrath," he said sympathetically. " I too was fond of the boy."

" It is incomprehensible," sighed Giebenrath. " He was so talented and everything was going well, school, examination—then, suddenly' one misfortune on top of another."

The shoemaker pointed at the frock-coated men as they disappeared through the cemetery gateway.

" There's a few of the gentlemen," he said in a quiet voice, " who have helped to drive him to this."

" What ? " said Giebenrath and he stared frightened and incredulous. " In the name of heaven, how ? "

" Don't worry, neighbour. I merely meant the school-masters."

" How do you mean exactly ? "

" Oh nothing. Just that. And you and I as well—don't you think that perhaps we failed the boy in many ways ? "

A serene blue sky extended over the small town; the river glistened in the valley; the pine-covered slopes showed as an attractive blue haze in the distance. The shoemaker smiled sadly. He took the arm of the man who was leaving behind him the stillness and strangely distressing thoughts that crowded in his mind, and was making his way back with hesitant, uneasy steps to the lower levels of his normal existence.

HERMANN HESSE Demian

Emil Sinclair boasts of a crime that he has not committed and subsequently finds himself blackmailed. Desperate, he turns to the mysterious Max Demian, in whom he finds a spiritual mentor, who leads him into a world of philosophical mysticism far removed from his everyday experience.

Peter Owen Modern Classic / 978-0-7206-1281-3

'Beautifully written, it has a seriousness as compelling as that of *The Waste Land* . . . the work of a major writer.' – *Observer*

HERMANN HESSE Gertrude

A disabled composer is drawn to a singer named Gertrude through their mutual love of music, falling hopelessly in love with her. But, because he fears arousing her sympathy instead of passion, he loses her. When she marries his friend he is compelled to stand by and watch as their obsessive relationship disintegrates into tragedy.

Peter Owen Modern Classic / 978-0-7206-1169-4

'It would be a pity to miss this book – it has such a rare flavour of beauty and simplicity.' – Stevie Smith

HERMANN HESSE The Journey to the East

The narrator of this allegorical tale travels through time and space in search of the ultimate truth. This pilgrimage to the 'East' covers both real and imagined lands and takes place not only in our own time but also in the Middle Ages and the Renaissance, encountering fellow travellers, both real and fictional, including Plato, Pythagoras, Don Quixote, Tristram Shandy and Baudelaire.

Peter Owen Modern Classic / 978-0-7206-1305-6

'A great writer . . . complex, subtle, allusive' – *New York Times Book Review*

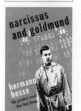

HERMANN HESSE Narcissus and Goldmund

Narcissus is a teacher at a monastery in medieval Germany and Goldmund his favourite pupil. While Narcissus remains detached from the world in prayer and meditation, Goldmund runs away in pursuit of love, living a picaresque life, his amatory adventures resulting in pain as well as ecstasy. His eventual reunion with his teacher brings into focus the diversity between artist and thinker, Dionysian and Apollonian.

Peter Owen Modern Classic / 978-0-7206-1291-2

'His greatest novel' – *New York Times*

HERMANN HESSE Peter Camenzind

This semi-autobiographical early novel gives a glimpse into the development of Hesse's beliefs. Camenzind, a Swiss peasant, becomes a university student and seems destined for academia. Instead, he seeks salvation through self-knowledge like a Romantic hero. But salvation proves elusive, and it is not until he returns to his own village that he can find the path that leads back to himself.

Peter Owen Modern Classic / 978-0-7206-1168-7

'One of the most penetrating accounts of a young man trying to discover the nature of his creative talent' – *Times Literary Supplement*

HERMANN HESSE Siddhartha

A special cased edition released to mark the fiftieth anniversary of Hesse's death, this is the classic tale of a rich man's spiritual journey to follow the teachings of the Buddha and discover the true meaning of existence.

With a foreword by Pico Iyer and an introduction by John Hughes

Cased / 978-0-7206-1482-4

'This book outlasts fashion and speaks to so many.' – Pico Iyer

PETER OWEN
MODERN CLASSICS

Since 1998 Peter Owen has been reissuing classic backlist fiction in the Peter Owen Modern Classics series. Currently numbering around ninety titles, the series brings together many of the greatest names from our sixty-plus years of publishing.

MODERN CLASSICS AUTHORS

Ryunosuke AKUTAGAWA, Li ANG, Guillaume APOLLINAIRE, Blaise CENDRARS, Marc CHAGALL, Jean COCTEAU, COLETTE, Machado de ASSIS, Lawrence DURRELL, Isabelle EBERHARDT, Shusaku ENDO, André GIDE, Jean GIONO, Alfred HAYES, Hermann HESSE, Anna KAVAN, Violette LEDUC, Yukio MISHIMA, Anaïs NIN, Boris PASTERNAK, Cesare PAVESE, Mervyn PEAKE, Marcel PROUST, Joseph ROTH, Cora SANDEL, Natsume SOSEKI, Gertrude STEIN, Bram STOKER, Tarjei VESAAS, Noel VIRTUE

 Peter Owen Publishers, 81 Ridge Road, London N8 9NP, UK
T + 44 (0)20 8350 1775 / F + 44 (0)20 8340 9488 / E info@peterowen.com
www.peterowen.com / @PeterOwenPubs
Independent publishers since 1951